Grizzly Creek Runs Red

Scott Harris, J.L Guin, Bruce Harris, Cheryl Pierson,
Tracy T. Thurman, Russ Towne,
'Big' Jim Williams, Nerissa Stacey, Justin Harris.
Plus a very special *guest author*!

ISBN: 9781731081155

Introduction

You may be familiar with the 500 Word Micro Short books that I've produced, along with 51 of my Western writing friends; The Shot Rang Out, A Dark & Stormy Night and Bourbon & A Good Cigar. Each of these books used a shared prompt and 52 writers used that prompt to write a 500-word Western short story.

As much fun as those books have been – and continue to be – some of the writers asked for a little more room, a few more words. So, Grizzly Creek Runs Red is an extension of those books, but this time we take the shared prompt....

The four had ridden themselves and their horses to exhaustion. They were out of food, water and patience and decided the time had come to quit running and take a stand.

... and nine of us have each written a 5,000 word short story. It gives us the luxury of a little more room to play, to develop characters and stories. These were a blast for us to write and I hope you enjoy reading them as much as we did writing them.

Western shorts live on!

Table of

Contents

The Best Hand Wins

By

J.L. Guin

Scott Harris

Emmett Cooper cast his eyes around as he and two others rode their horses down the main street of the little town known as Findley, so named after the first man to file a claim on the nearby creek. When word got out about the sizeable amount of Findley's find, a horde of starry-eyed miners rushed to the spot to stake a claim. Soon after, a town began to form and had grown over the years following.

Miguel Contreras, age twenty-eight, was the first to nose his horse, next to two others, at a hitch rail fronting a clothing store next to the bank. Regis Thornton, age thirty, was next. Their leader, Emmett Cooper, age forty, last in line, nosed his horse to the rail. Randall Gibbs, age twenty-one, stood on the boardwalk fronting the hitch rail. Across the street, Billy Wilkes, age twenty, milled about the boardwalk fronting the A-1 hardware store.

The men's timely arrival and positions were planned and agreed upon last night, in Murphy's Saloon, located in Jefferson, a neighboring town some ten miles to the north.

During the evening at a card table, Regis Thornton became impressed with how Randall Gibbs, a cocky young gambler, outwitted and outwaited the other gamblers to be the big winner of the night. At the end of the game, only Gibbs and Thornton remained at the table.

Thornton seemed curious about the young gambler's abilities. The two talked for a time while Gibbs counted his winnings.

"You are pretty good with the cards," Thornton said. "What else do you do?"

Gibbs grinned then began bragging about his abilities with not only cards but his six-gun as well. Thornton soon learned from the seemingly slightly inebriated Gibbs that he did not hold a regular job but managed to get by mostly on his card winnings. Gibbs mentioned that his abilities at coming out a winner at the tables sometimes called for a sleight of hand.

Thornton grinned, then asked, "What do you do for money, if on occasion, you go broke?"

Gibbs answered coolly, "Then I use my six-gun to get what I want."

At that time, Billy Wilkes, a young cowboy, walked up and seated himself at the table. "Looks like you took those suckers for a good pot, Randall. Long as you're fat with cash, I could use a couple bucks till payday."

"Connie putting the bite on you again, Billy?" Gibbs asked.

Wilkes nodded. "I don't know what she does with what money I give her, but she always acts like she doesn't have a dime."

Gibbs reached to the tabletop and flipped two one-dollar coins to land in front of the cowboy. Wilkes scooped up the coins, dropped them into a shirt pocket, then headed to the bar to get some beer.

Gibbs shook his head, then said to Thornton, "The damn fool lets that whore bleed him dry. I tried to tell him she was no good, but he won't listen to what I say. He went ahead and moved in with her and her kid about two months ago. She quit the saloon and has been working on him ever since, seems like daily. She takes everything he makes and wants more. He told me that she even suggested that he ought to see about taking on a night time job, saloon swamping if need be, as well as his day work till things got better."

"What kind of work does he do?" Thornton asked.

Gibbs grimaced. "Whatever comes to hand, I guess. He ain't got a regular job. Does deliveries for the mercantile, a little work for a local ranch when there is a need, mostly shit jobs that the monthly hands shun. Billy is a good gun hand, but since he moved in with that woman, he's at her beck and call. He gives everything he makes to her. She gives him back something like 10 to 25 cents a day, just enough for a couple beers and a sack of tobacco."

Thornton nodded. "Everybody is looking to get ahead, I reckon."

Gibbs puffed a cigar to life then squinted one eye as the smoke swirled around his head. "What brings you and your friends to Jefferson? None of you look like working cowboys to me."

Thornton grinned. "Pretty sharp of you to notice the small things, Randall. It's as you say, we don't work cattle. We generally do as you say you do at times. We use our six-guns to take what we want."

Gibbs grinned. "Anything lined up that you might need a little help with? The locals are getting a little too wise to the way I do things."

Thornton nodded. "Information mostly, but we wouldn't be opposed to an extra hand or so to get a job done."

Gibbs stared at Thornton. "I'm your man," he said, then added, "If you need more men, Billy will do anything that I ask of him."

Thornton nodded. "Good, good. My friends and I believe the bank over in Findley has a pile of money in the safe that is waiting for a withdrawal. We need to know about Findley, what kind of law they got. What time does the bank open? What kind of guards they got and such."

At that time, Billy Wilkes appeared at the table with a pitcher of beer in hand. "Drink up, men."

Gibbs waited until Billy took a chair then introduced him to Thornton and said, "Got a deal going the next day or so. Could be a good payday if you can get away."

Billy nodded and sat up straight then placed a hand to his six-gun but did not draw it. "Ain't anybody got a hold on me. When it comes to money, I'm ready to do what it takes to get some."

When Gibbs began reciting the answers to Thornton's questions, Thornton held up a hand. "Hold on for a minute. It would be best if you told what you know about Findley and the bank to my partners as well as me." With that said, he stood and led the way to Emmett Cooper and Miguel Contreras's table. Gibbs and Billy Wilkes followed.

After introductions, the group sat until past midnight.

Emmett Cooper was not at all thrilled with the new additions, especially the fact that they were so young and appeared too eager. Cooper had been stealing his way through life for the past fifteen years after the defeat of the Confederate Army when he was twenty years old. Upon returning home, he found no opportunities for work in Arkansas. He figured to find something, so he headed west and south into Texas and ended up doing ranch work then trail driving for each of the next five years.

At the end of his last trail drive to Colorado, he held his pay—ninety-two dollars in his hand. He was now out of work until next spring, a good five or six months away, and ninety-two dollars sure as hell would not last that long. He could ride back to Texas with the chuck wagon and eat the ranch's provided grub, but once he got there, he knew the owner would cut him loose. He knew he needed to do something—that there had to be a better way of making a living.

Emmett preferred to cut loose now, which he did. He soon found that any work available in town paid less than cattle droving. It was a hand-to-mouth existence, so he began prowling around at night, when others slept. He found it easy to steal things that he could sell later. After a time, he tired of having to sneak to sell, at less than realistic prices, whatever he had stolen. That prompted him to try other things.

He planned and pulled his first robbery on a dark section of road some ten miles from the nearest town. He masked his face then rode his horse to block the road and held up a stagecoach. A whole thirty-two dollars and some loose change from the three passengers was the entire take.

The thing about Emmett Cooper was that he was a thief for sure, but he had never killed anyone, other than during the war, and he wanted to keep it that way. For one, those he pointed a six-gun at almost always cowed and allowed him to have his way, thus no need for gunplay. The rewards offered on him were so minimal, no bounty hunter would bother pursuing him, particularly because those he had robbed could not supply an accurate description of the masked man riding a sorrel horse. The other thing was, he learned that those who shot people ended up with a big reward offered on their heads, and they had to run like hell to stay ahead of the law. Those caught up with were either shot on sight or died at the end of a rope.

His two long time partners, Regis Thornton and Miguel Contreras, knew this and preferred to operate under Emmett's leadership in a like manner, which was robbing and stealing without gun violence. Past crimes had proven to them that large or small communities would cut their losses and soon forget about the money taken as long as no one got hurt. This job, if his information was correct regarding the amount of money in the bank, would be the largest haul that he and his partners had attempted. He wanted it to go off without a hitch, and an extra man would make sense, someone to watch their backs while they took care of business. Two extra men seemed a stretch, but now that the new arrivals knew what was up, he relented.

It was late at night, perhaps after a few too many drinks, that Emmett agreed to take the two newcomers into the gang. He did not particularly like Billy Wilkes from the start; the mouthy kid seemed to be spoiling for a fight. In whispers, Thornton assured him that Gibbs would hold Wilkes in check.

Thornton and Contreras both grinned when Emmett began to instruct the two new arrivals. "Look, it's like this: We're here to rob the bank in Findley. If everything goes okay, we will be out of there in no time without firing a shot. It is okay to show your weapon, wave it around, but there is no need to shoot or kill anyone. If it comes to shooting, aim for the ground or over their heads and spook them into taking cover. A shot or two hitting a doorway or the ground in front of someone will make him think twice about getting involved."

Scott Harris

Chapter Two

At first light, Emmett, Regis and Miguel assembled at the livery where they had left their horses. Since they had paid in advance, the livery owner had told them that the door would be open and they could get their animals whenever they wanted. They quickly saddled their mounts then led them down the street to Emma's Cafe, where a single kerosene lamp glowed inside. The men tied their mounts then stepped inside the cafe. They were the first customers.

"It will take a few minutes for the coffee to boil," Emma, a big-boned, round woman informed them and then busied herself lighting additional lamps.

A little while later, Emma filled each coffee cup then took the men's breakfast orders.

When served, the men ate their breakfasts silently while waiting for Randall Gibbs and Billy Wilkes to arrive. By the time they had finished the meal of eggs, potatoes and hot biscuits, Gibbs and Wilkes rode to the front of the building. The three seated men wasted no time, swallowed the last of their coffee, stood, left money enough for the meals and a generous tip on the table then stepped outside.

The men nodded greetings to the still-mounted Gibbs and Wilkes then swung into their own saddles. The five men walked their horses out of town before nudging the animals to a lope. They spent the next two hours riding toward Findley.

Emmett Cooper brought his horse to a stop on a hill overlooking the one street town some five hundred yards distant. The four others crowded their horses to stand alongside Emmett's horse. For the most part, the street appeared empty, which was just the way they wanted it. Like most mining towns, many of the men were already out on their claims or still sleeping off the effects of last night's revelry.

Emmitt commented, "I figure we're a bit early yet, if that bank opens at nine, like you say, Randall. You and Billy can go ahead and ride in first, tie up to that hitch rail in front of the store on the left side of the bank. Billy, you walk across the street to the front of that mercantile, look at some tools and such and keep watch from there. Randall, you stay with the horses, fiddle around looking at a hoof like there is a problem. When you see that the bank is open for business, raise your hat above your head, so that we can see it," Emmett instructed. "Miguel, Regis and I will ride in once you two are in place and Randall gives the signal."

Billy Wilkes lifted his bandana up to cover his nose. Emmett Cooper noticed the move and gave a quick reprimand to the young man of twenty, half Emmett's age. "No need for that yet, Billy. We do not want to advertise what is going on until the last minute. You can mask your face once you see that we are going inside the bank. Your job is to cover our backs, give a wave of the hand to Randall if you see something out of line. Do not let some do-good merchant come outside with a scattergun in his hand. Just keep watch, and once you see the door open and we start out, then run like hell to your horse and get mounted up."

Emmett looked across the street to where Billy Wilkes was pacing around. He then nodded to Randall Gibbs that everything looked okay. "Stay with the horses and let us know if anyone comes snooping. If so, get the drop on them but don't let them come in the bank," he told the younger man.

Emmett, Regis and Miguel all pulled bandanas up over their noses then filled a hand with a six-gun, stepped to the bank's entrance and filed in. The three robbers were carrying out a routine that they had done on several occasions. Emmett would go in first, followed by Regis. They would take care of the bank employees and do the actual handling of the money, while Miguel Contreras took a position by the door to stand watch for any threats from outside.

It was Emmett's job to announce their intentions, which he did in a loud voice as soon as he stepped through the door. "This is a holdup! Do as you are told and no one gets hurt!" He held a six-gun chest high, while sweeping his eyes and the muzzle of the six-gun around the room.

Regis quickly stepped past Emmett to a short fenced-in area connected to a counter and a teller's cage. A tall, skinny fellow in a black suit stepped from behind the teller cage. Upon hearing and seeing what was going on, he stood stock-still and thrust his hands toward the ceiling.

Regis tossed a bag to the teller. "Fill that up. We want it all."

The teller caught the bag, stepped back to the cage, and began emptying the contents of the drawer into the sack.

Regis stepped over the fence just as a suited, portly man stepped from an adjoining room— most likely the bank manager's office. Regis pointed his six-gun at the wide-eyed man's face, which suddenly paled.

"Where's the safe?" Regis growled.

The man pointed to the room that he had just exited. "In there," he said, and then added, "but I haven't opened it yet."

There was an audible click as Regis cocked the six-gun he held on the man. The man's eyes grew larger. "Please, sir, there is no need for that; we'll do as you say. I don't want anyone to get hurt."

"Open it!" Regis demanded. The man nodded his head then turned and stepped back into the office. He knelt on one knee before the big Baldwin safe situated on the back wall. He took hold of the dial and turned two spins right, one left, then one to the right. He put his hand to the handle and opened the safe door then stood and stepped back.

Regis pushed the man aside then knelt on one knee. He pulled a canvas sack from his belt and began filling it with the stacks of bills within. When satisfied that he had all the paper money, he lifted a pair of foot-high bags of coins from the safe's bottom shelf and thought of depositing those into his sack as well but dismissed the idea, as they were too cumbersome to handle on horseback.

"Is that all of it?" Regis asked.

The manager nodded. "Yes, that is all. We are not withholding anything."

When Regis stepped back over the little inside fence, Emmett told the manager and teller, "Get on the floor and put your hands behind your head. Do not get up or say anything until we are gone. You do as I say and you won't get hurt."

Emmett was pleased; so far, things were going well with no disruptions. That all changed when he and the others began filing out the front door. Across the street, Billy Wilkes had just stepped onto the street when a voice behind him called out, "Hey, what's going on there?"

Billy, with his bandana masking his face and his six-gun in hand, whirled around to see a tall man with an apron around his middle and a shotgun in hand standing on the boardwalk where Billy had just stepped. Billy's immediate response was to bring his six-gun to bear on the man. That proved a mistake on his part, for when he began to swing his six-gun around, the man on the boardwalk leveled the double-barreled shotgun toward Billy.

The shotgun's boom sounded a fraction of second before Billy pulled the trigger of his six-gun. Both shots scored hits. The aproned man, hit high on the left side of his shoulder by the .45 bullet, fell to the boardwalk but rolled over quickly to put himself behind a barrel of axe handles. A cloud of gun smoke from his own expended round hovered in the air just above where he lay. One-handed, he swung the shotgun back toward his adversary but there was no need. Billy Wilkes lay motionless, dead, sprawled on his back in the street where he had landed after the load of buckshot had obliterated his stomach and intestines. The gun smoke from the expended round of Billy's six-gun drifted lazily in the air a few feet in front of and above the body.

Across the street, Emmett, Regis and Miguel hurried to their horses while Randall Gibbs, hunched in a crouch to the left of the horses, held his six-gun trained to where he had just witnessed Billy Wilkes falling to the ground. Regis tossed the sack of money to Emmett, who busied securing it to his saddle horn then he, Regis and Miguel all swung into their saddles. Emmett looked over to Randall Gibbs, who was still staring at the motionless body of his friend, Billy, lying in the street.

"He's done for. Get mounted," Emmett commanded.

At that moment, the door to the bank opened and the suited manager began squalling from the doorway, "Holdup! Holdup! They're robbing the bank!"

Randall Gibbs turned to face the man then reacted by pulling the trigger of his six-gun twice. Both shots hit the manager high up on his chest. When the man fell back inside the bank, Gibbs stepped away to swing into his saddle. By this time, doors up and down the street opened and men with guns in hand were stepping onto the street.

Shots sounded. Miguel Contreras slumped in his saddle when a bullet hit him in the back of his left arm. Emmett and Regis began firing their six-guns in the direction of the men filling the street, in hopes of spooking them to take cover. The men scattered without taking any hits. A lone man quick walking from across the street began firing a six-gun at the men. Randall Gibbs emptied his six-gun at the man and scored a hit on the last shot. With spurs gouging their sides, the four men's horses thundered out of town back the way they had come.

Once out of sight of the town, Emmett slowed his horse to a stop. The others grouped up beside him.

"You hit bad, Miguel?" Emmett asked.

Miguel shook his head. "Hurts like hell, but I'll make it."

Emmett stepped his horse beside Miguel's mare. "Let me see." He wrapped his reins around his saddle horn then took both hands to Miguel's arm and shirt to inspect. He took the bloody material in hand and ripped the sleeve around and off.

Emmett looked at both sides of Miguel's arm. "The bullet didn't hit the bone. Went clear through, but the holes need to be bound up, else you might bleed out."

Miguel, with his uninjured arm, undid his bandana and handed it to Emmett.

Emmett shook out the bandana, wrapped the arm tightly and tied the ends. He then took off his own bandana and tied it around Miguel's neck, fashioning a sling. "Put your hand and arm in here to keep the pressure off. We'll do a better job of fixing things tonight in camp."

Miguel used his right hand to lift his left hand and forearm into the sling.

"You think they'll follow?" Randall Gibbs asked.

Emmett turned to glare at the young man. "You and Billy shooting those men guaranteed it," he said with disdain, then added, "From the looks of that group, I'd say they'll be a bunch of them on our heels before long."

"That man at the bank surprised me," Randall Gibbs cut in. "I wasn't aiming to kill him."

"Then why did you shoot him the second time?" Emmett expelled angrily.

Gibbs shook his head. "Well... I—" he stammered.

Emmett cut him off. "What's done is done. We need to ride like hell and put some distance behind us."

Scott Harris

Chapter Three

Findley's town Marshal Arch Wiggins, a tough 38-year-old longtime lawman, was struggling to get up from the street where he had fallen when Randall Gibbs emptied his six-gun at him. The last shot had hit the meaty part of Wiggin's left thigh. Luckily for the marshal, the bullet had gone through without hitting the bone or an artery.

Fred Conti, the mercantile owner holding his own wounded shoulder with his good hand, was first to reach him. "How bad are you hit, Arch?"

"My leg is holed but I'll be okay soon as Doc Grimes sews me up. Need to get a posse and get after those bastards."

Milt Watkins, the barber, walked up with a six-gun still in hand. "I winged one of them," he said.

"Good," the marshal said. By that time, eight other townsmen had walked up. "Help me up," Wiggins said to no one in particular. Two men helped the marshal to his feet. Once on his feet and supported by the two men, the marshal asked, "Anybody know who they are? Have you seen any of them around town of late?"

"That one lying in the street is named Billy. I don't know his last name, from over in Jefferson," Fred Conti said. "I saw him out at the Star Ranch when I was making a delivery."

A man standing in the group said, "That other one that shot you and the banker is most likely Randall Gibbs, a no-account that spends all his time gambling in the saloons. I have seen him and Billy together at the saloon over in Jefferson. If that is the same Billy, then his last name is Wilkes. He ain't got a regular job. Lives with a whore and does odd jobs around town, as far as I know."

Wiggins nodded his understanding, "What about those other three? Anyone know who they are?"

Only Fred Conti answered, "They had their faces covered with masks. Maybe Wilson, the teller, got a better look than any of us did."

"I'll have a word with him soon as I get patched up," Wiggins said then turned his head and spoke to a tall man to his right, with a deputy badge on his shirtfront. "Luther, need you to get our horses then get us outfitted for a two-to-three-day outing. We'll be going after those bastards right soon." He raised his voice. "Anybody wanting to go along, I'll deputize you. Just make sure you got a good horse, a good gun and are willing to do as I tell you."

Chapter Four

Emmett Cooper spurred his horse to a full run and the others followed suit. Emmett's mind was active as he rode along. He had never been in a situation like this with what he figured would be a mad as hell posse dogging his trail. Starting with that first stage holdup he'd done single-handedly, he'd always ridden away from his thefts easily and never worried much about being followed. In part, it was because he carefully planned every robbery, taking advantage only when the timing was right. Stealth and darkness had always been his ally, but that was when he worked alone. Thornton and Contreras were good, loyal comrades, always doing as he directed. Neither had ever caused a problem. The three had operated efficiently, taking what they wanted without being recognized. They had never been in a situation that forced them to run from a posse.

The problems arose when he agreed to take on those two newcomers, Billy Wilkes and Randall Gibbs. He did not blame Thornton for bringing them to the table last night. The blame rested totally on his own shoulders for allowing two unknowns, who appeared full of themselves to begin with, to come along on the biggest score of his career.

Regis Thornton brought his horse alongside Emmett's speeding mount. Thornton held out his hand, motioning with a palm down to slow down. "We're gonna kill these horses if we keep up this pace," Thornton said.

Emmett pulled back on the reins a little and brought his horse slowly down to a walk.

"You are right, Regis. I guess I got in a bit of a hurry. Let's see if we can find some water and shade for a while."

They found a trickling creek and a shaded spot hidden from distant view. They slid from their horses and allowed them to drink a bit before pulling up the animals' noses for fear of the horses bloating themselves. Miguel lingered at the creek and began bathing his arm while Emmett assisted. Regis led his and the other men's horses to a grassy area.

Emmett again inspected Miguel's wounded arm. "Looks okay, Miguel, but them holes ought to be sewed shut. For now, the best we can do is to bind it up again until we can find a doctor to take care of it." Miguel nodded as Emmett washed out the bandana then retied it around Miguel's arm. The men sat in the shade for ten minutes while their horses rested some.

Randall Gibbs rolled a smoke then asked, "How much you figure is in the sack, Emmett?

Emmett gave him a cold stare. "There will be time for counting after we make some tracks out of this section of the country. It doesn't take long for a bunch of mad as hell townsmen to form a posse."

Gibbs shrugged a shoulder. "Might take longer than usual. That one that fell in the street was the marshal. His deputy ain't much to worry about. I've had words with him before. He's green as a board."

Emmett was seething with anger at the young smartass, but he held his tongue in check. There would be time to deal with him later.

Emmett knelt by the creek then splashed water onto his face. "Well, I aim to find a high spot and get a look at our back trail, that way we'll know for sure."

After a few minutes, Emmett walked to his horse, mounted up, then said, "You live in this country, Randall. Which way do we go?"

Randall pointed to the left. "If you want to get up high, head that way."

"Let's go," Emmett said.

An hour later, after topping out a hill, Emmett pulled his horse to a stop and pulled an expanding telescope from a saddlebag. He studied their back trail, lingering for a time on one area. He handed the telescope to Regis Thornton. "Tell me what you see, Regis."

Regis Thornton studied for a time then handed the scope back to Emmett. "Looks like a bit of dust kicked up to me. At least a dozen or so, I'd say. They are right on our trail. We need to shag."

The four bank robbers rode on under a sliver of a moon in a clear sky. By two a.m., they and their horses needed rest.

"Let's find a place we can watch our back trail and get some rest," Emmett said.

When the first hint of light began showing on the eastern horizon, Regis Thornton walked over to where Emmett was curled up on the ground. He bent over and gave Emmett's shoulder a nudge. "Company's coming, Emmett. They'll be here in an hour or sooner."

Emmett sat upright with his eyes widened as he stared at Regis, who in turn grimaced then confirmed, "For sure," he said. "They must have tracked us all night without taking a rest."

Emmett had to shake Miguel's good shoulder three times to arouse the man. He was pale and sweating profusely with a fever. When asked if he was okay, Miguel nodded. "I'll be all right."

It was a mad scramble to catch up the horses. Emmett and Regis worked together to saddle their mounts as well as Miguel's, while Randall saddled his own. In a short time, the four were heading out.

It was a cat and mouse chase all that day and into the night with the posse dogging their trail but not seeming to gain on them. The four weary men chewed what jerky they had and drank their canteens empty while in the saddle. On the high ground, there were no streams available to water the horses. Emmett as well as Randall gouged their horse's flanks with their spurs to keep the tired animals moving.

Before dawn the next morning, Miguel fell from his saddle. Emmett and Regis both jumped from their saddles and rushed to the downed man's side. He was out cold, pale and barely breathing. There was no response when Emmett shook him, while calling his name.

"What are we going to do, Emmett?" Regis asked in dismay. "They are real close. I can hear their horses coming along."

Emmett glared at him while Randall crowded close to see what was going on.

The four had ridden themselves and their horses to exhaustion. They were out of food, water and patience and decided that the time had come to quit running and take a stand.

Emmett Cooper knew the gig was up, but he was not going down without a fight. "Help me get Miguel over his saddle. We need to get to the top of this ridge so we can hold them off come daylight.

It was a struggle to force the horses the last few yards to the top just as gray dawn began lighting up the ridgetop. Emmett and Regis both took a hand in getting Miguel off his horse and lain out behind an outcropping of rocks. Emmett took a canteen in hand in hope to wipe Miguel's face, but there was no water left. He sighed in dismay.

Regis walked away to look around and see if there was a way to continue. He came back a few minutes later. "Hate to tell you this, Emmett, but as far as I can tell, the only way off this mountain is back the way we came. We're sitting at the top of a ledge with nothing but drop-offs on three sides."

Emmett stared at his partner in dismay. He did not say anything but nodded his understanding of the situation.

A few minutes later, Randall Gibbs stepped to where Emmett was kneeling beside Miguel. "I spotted some smoke and a fire down the hill where we came up. It looks to me like they are setting up camp and fixing breakfast."

Emmett nodded. "They have us right where they want us."

"You think they will rush us?" Gibbs asked while pulling his six-gun and checking the loads.

Emmett shook his head. "No need to. They do not have to fire a shot, Randall." He paused for a moment then said, "It's just like in cards. The best hand wins."

Gibbs stared at him in wonder.

Emmett then said, "They got food, water and ridable horses, and we're sitting here with none of that and nowhere to go. All they have to do is wait us out."

The End

Scott Harris

No Corpse for the Coffin

by

Bruce Harris

Scott Harris

The four had ridden themselves and their horses to exhaustion. They were out of food, water and patience and decided the time had come to quit running and take a stand. Beverly Diamond took charge. She raised a hand. Her once polished and manicured red nail polish was now badly chipped from the long ordeal.

"Enough!" she commanded, glancing sideways at Clem Stallings. Clem lay belly-side down across a worn leather saddle, the circular bloodstain on the back of his pants leg increased several inches in circumference since the last time Beverly peeked at Clem. "Look it him." She pointed at Clem. "He isn't going to make it."

"None of us are!" chided Sally Newsome, tears streaming down her once-rouged cheeks. Her red silk dress, perfectly matched with that of Jane Taylor's, was mud-stained and tattered along the hem. Jane, the fourth member of the group, was thankful Beverly had called them to a stop. Jane, not sure she could go another few feet, felt nauseated and weak.

*****

Beverly Diamond, real name Beverly Diamante, could sing. Back in New Mexico, she had gotten her first singing job after changing her name to Beverly Diamond. "No one comes into a saloon to hear a Beverly Diamante," exclaimed Burt Matthews, owner of the Golden Coin Saloon. He removed a sodden cigar from his mouth and pointed it at Beverly. "But lots of people would want to hear Beverly Diamond." Matthews was correct. Beverly's voice did the rest. The crowds and her career grew, until she wound up singing in large halls in San Francisco, met and married a no-good gambler who abused her a year after the marriage and nearly got her killed when the bum got involved with the wrong people. The couple fell into debt, and Beverly found herself alone one April day. After failing to collect what they were owed, a couple of "friends" deposited Beverly's dead husband at the door of the couple's ranch. A knife stuck into his back pierced a handwritten note. It read:

LEAVE THIS HOUSE - YOU GOT 24 HOURS

She ripped the letter from her husband's body, tore it to shreds and cursed. There was never a decision. Beverly had no intention of testing the killers' resolve and gamble with her own life. She did what the letter ordered—took off and never looked back. She figured the house was a cheap way to even the score for her husband's debts. It seemed a lifetime ago. She made her own way, eventually settling in Nevada, where she had steady work as a singer at a saloon called the Grizzly Creek. Clem Stallings accompanied her on piano. Sally Newsome and Jane Taylor danced and served drinks.

*****

Still wearing her blue silk dress, Beverly, the two women and the badly wounded Clem

Stallings had ridden for hours, mostly in the dark. Beverly said, "We got to stop. This horse can't take another step, and I don't know about the rest of you but I'm weak and tired. I just want to cry. And sleep."

"If we stop now, Clem's sure to die," said Jane Taylor. She glanced Clem. She imagined blood dripping into and accumulating in his boots. She shuddered.

"Don't matter," responded Sally Newsome. "We're all about to die."

Beverly looked around. She pointed to an opening in the brush. "Let's rest here. We've got a few hours. They'll probably wait till dawn before tracking us down."

"When they do, they're going to kill us anyway," spat Jane Taylor. "We need a sheriff."

Beverly shrugged. "Sure, if we find one, we'll be sure to let him know. We're on our own."

"And at this point, I don't care," snapped Jane.

"Shut up!" screamed Beverly, quickly apologizing. "We're not going to die. We didn't come this far to simply give up and die."

Taylor sniggered. Clem Stallings had passed out hours ago. Sally Newsome spoke. "Jane's right. We have no chance. They'll catch up to us and find us and kill us. We've seen them. We know their faces. We can identify them. They won't let us live."

"We won't let them kill us!" countered Diamond. "After a little rest, we'll face the consequences and fight back."

"And how are we going to stop them?" asked Newsome.

"It's four against two," answered Beverly.

"Ha!" shouted Jane Taylor. "Four against two? You're including him?" She nodded toward Clem Stallings. "He'll be dead before those two find us. And how do you think the three of us, three women with no weapons, can defend ourselves against two outlaws who we know have no problem with killing? Or did you see something different than me last night back in Grizzly Creek?"

*****

Grizzly Creek. Saturday. The ranch-hands from Otis Radburn's OR Ranch packed the saloon. Most had worked five and a half days, getting off early on Saturday as was Otis Radburn's practice and why cowpokes coveted working for Mr. Radburn. Saturday. Money to burn at the Grizzly Creek, and despite the early hour of the evening, every table was taken and it was two-deep standing room at the curved, ornate bar. Radburn was a shrewd businessman. In addition to running the ranch, he owned a significant piece of the Grizzly Creek. After his ranch hands had their night on the town, Radburn recouped most of the wages he paid out. In addition, he protected his interest in the Grizzly Creek saloon by forbidding weapons inside. Guns, rifles, ammunition and you name it had to be checked at the door before entering the establishment. Radburn knew alcohol and guns don't mix, and he wanted to ensure the place didn't get shot up every weekend. Unfortunately, word about Grizzly Creek's gun policy was out, and two brothers, Jed and Pit Bailey, fresh out of jail, had ideas. Others had tried to rob the place before them, but none had succeeded thanks to the watchful eyes of Sheriff Martin Brinkman and his Deputy Colt McCracken. Both lawmen, however, were taken by surprise after Pit Bailey tossed a stick of dynamite in front of the town bank. The Bailey brothers ambushed Brinkman and McCracken and stormed into the Grizzly Creek. Beverly Diamond was mid-song when the first shots rang out. The brothers said nothing. They spoke with bullets. Blood splattered across drinks, cards, tables, belts, boots, and the floor. Reflexively, the startled customers reached to their hips for their weapons, but holsters were empty. Given their various drunken states, all were helpless. Radburn himself was in the saloon that evening and took lead to his chest.

Among the chaos, piano player Clem Stallings grabbed Beverly's arm. "Let's get out of here now! I know a way. Follow me, quick!"

The two servers, Sally Newsome and Jane Taylor, saw Stallings and Diamond and followed them out.

"Don't look back!" ordered Stallings. "Just do as..." and he dropped to the floor. Beverly's scream went unheard. It mixed in with the others' shouts and cries for help.

"Are you okay?" she asked Stallings.

"My leg. Just keep going. Let's go! I'll make it. There are a couple of horses behind the fence. The ones old Chester Plummer plans to auction off Monday."

"You're bleeding," said Jane.

Limping badly, Clem Stallings managed to get himself out of the Grizzly Creek and onto a horse. The three women, still dressed in their silk dresses, followed. "It was them damn Bailey brothers doing that. They'll hang for this." Pain shot through his leg. He grimaced.

"They saw us, Clem," said Beverly. "They'll surely come after us."

Gritting his teeth, Clem answered, "Yup. But we'll get a good start on them. By the time they finish up in there and take everyone's money, we'll be far away. Hopefully, they'll wait till morning. Just keep moving. Don't stop and don't worry about me. I'll be fine."

*****

Beverly Diamond, Sally Newsome, and Jane Taylor worked together removing Clem Stallings from his horse and tried to make the unconscious man as comfortable as possible. For several minutes, no one spoke. They were all too tired and hungry. Stallings' chest rose and lowered slowly, irregularly. Life continued to seep out from the bullet hole in his leg. Beverly sighed. "I say we get some sleep, restore our energy and be ready for them."

"And then what?" asked Newsome. "I'd rather die in my sleep without food or water in my stomach than face those two with a full belly. Nope. If I get to sleep, and I don't think I'll have any trouble given as tired as I am, I'm fixing to stay asleep and figure to wake up in heaven or hell. Whichever don't matter to me now. This sure feels like hell anyways."

"I know where I'll wake up," said Jane Taylor. "I better shed some clothing. It's going to be a might hotter when I wake up. Really hot."

The horses moped. It was as if they too had lost all interest. Suddenly, Beverly Diamond stared at Taylor. "What did you say, Jane?"

"About what? Dying? I said it's going to be hot when—"

"No," interrupted Diamond. "About your clothes. Shedding your clothes."

Jane Taylor yawned. It was contagious. Sally Newsome broke into full yawn before Jane's was finished. "I don't know… oh… shed my clothing? That? It was a joke. Ha-ha."

Beverly Diamond snapped her fingers. "That's it. I have a plan." The two other women looked at her, then each other, and then stared back at Diamond. "Listen, we first get some sleep. Best we can. That'll give us a little strength. There are two of them. Men." She paused. No response from either Newsome or Taylor, so Beverly continued. "Men. We're women."

Sally Newsome interjected and turned toward Jane Taylor. "I think she's gone crazy. I can't listen to this. We're all about to be killed."

"Women!" screamed Beverly in a voice that even surprised her. "Attractive women. When those two approach, the two of you… you know… display some feminine charm. Shed some clothing… distract them." Beverly saw interest in her two friends' faces. "While they have their filthy minds on you, I'll whack them with a rock.

There must be some good ones around here." She turned and searched the ground.

"You're crazy, Beverly. That will never work," said Sally.

"You got a better idea? Either of you? Once I strike one, you two attack the other until I can hit him with the rock as well. It's our only chance."

Exhausted, Jane Taylor gave in. "Fine. I can't go on at this point. We're doomed anyway."

Resigned, Sally Newsome nodded agreement. Beverly glanced over at Clem Stallings. He was still alive, but it wouldn't be for much longer. The three women got as comfortable as possible and closed their eyes. None of them thought sleep was possible, but the sheer magnitude of their long journey had taken its toll. Within minutes the three slept, while two murderous outlaws decided not to wait until dawn and rode closer.

*****

God's face. Beverly opened her eyes, shut them, and reopened them again. She never really thought too much about God during her lifetime. No one, she figured, had ever looked after her well-being, especially no higher authority. But, if she were asked to describe what she thought the image of the Lord would be, this was it, staring down at her with two dark chocolate-brown eyes, concern in his face, with a long, flowing beard. Beverly tried to remember if the two Bailey brothers had found her and killed her, or if the lack of food and water had done her in. She didn't think about the others—Clem, Sally, or Jane. She was self-focused. She wanted to ask the question, "Heaven or hell?" but was too afraid. She studied the face in front of her. Human-like. She remembered some scripture from her childhood. Something about being made in God's image. She never read the Bible, didn't believe in that sort of thing. Now, she wished she had. She figured her odds would be better now that one life was done and the second—the one for eternity—had begun. "Is this heaven or hell?" she asked, the words uncontrollably spilling from her cracked, dry lips.

A broad smile creased the man's face. He reached out and gently touched Beverly's forehead. "This is Nevada," he said. "Please, take some water."

Beverly sat up and sipped, gulped, and choked. "Easy now," the man said. "Slowly."

Beverly rested her head again. "Did you say Nevada? So, this is heaven?"

"Some people think so. Others, not so much. Rest now. When you feel stronger, we will talk more."

But Beverly Diamond was having none of that. She sat up. "My friends... where are they? Where am I? Please!" She glanced around and noticed Sally and Jane still asleep in beds on opposite walls of a sparsely decorated room. "Where's Clem?" she cried. "Clem Stallings. There was a man with us. Clem Stallings. He was shot and..."

"Your friend lost a lot of blood. We pray that he will be okay."

"Who are you?" Beverly finally asked. "Where am I?"

"Forgive me. Of course, you are confused and scared. My name is Rabbi Solomon. This is—"

"You're not God?" an incredulous Beverly asked.

The rabbi chuckled. "Not at all. I'm a man of God, just like everyone else on this earth. This is my home. I lead a small congregation of Jews in these parts. We settled here years ago, coming from the East. A few of us heard noises from a horse and went to welcome our visitor. We found you and your friends sleeping. You all appeared to be in need of help. We carefully carried you and transferred you to my home. My wife has some bread and coffee."

Beverly saw a short woman holding a platter and a cup. She sat up, chewed bread and drank the hot coffee. Both Sally and Jane stirred at the same time. Rabbi Solomon went over to them and explained who he was and why the two were in his home. After a few minutes, all three women had eaten.

"Where's Clem? Our friend who was shot?" asked Beverly.

"One of our congregation members is a local doctor. He removed the bullet from your friend's leg, but as I told you, your friend is very ill. He's in the doctor's home just up the trail a way from here. We pray for him."

"Oh, my gosh. How long have we been asleep?" asked Beverly.

"A few hours. Why? What kind of trouble are you in? Can we help?"

"That's real nice of you," said Jane Taylor. "But unless you got some firearms here, guns and rifles and bullets, there's probably not much you can do to help us except give us some fresh horses so we can keep moving."

"I'm afraid we don't keep any weapons here. Horses we can provide, but what are you running away from?" asked Rabbi Solomon.

"That's great," said Newsome. "We're done running. It's back to Beverly's rock idea. How much time you think we have left before they show up?"

Beverly explained their plight to the rabbi and his wife, everything from the shootout at the Grizzly Creek to their long, arduous journey, to their plan of fighting off the two Bailey brothers. "The way I figure it," said Beverly, "there's really no telling when they'll be here."

"Hmmm," muttered Rabbi Solomon. "We don't have much time. I have faith and do not fear death, yet it might prove difficult reasoning with those two if they are as lawless and murderous as you've painted them."

"And worse," added Beverly.

"Okay then. I have an idea. It isn't exactly kosher, but I think it will provide the best outcome where no one gets hurt and we can all move on with our lives."

"I hope you're a magician rabbi," said Jane. "Because without guns, they'll kill us for certain, as well as you and your wife, and not think twice about it."

The rabbi addressed his wife. He barked orders and she rushed off. "You three stay here. We haven't a moment to lose. We have to act quickly." With that, Rabbi Solomon sped out the door.

Four plots were dug. Men stood with shovels, wiping their brows. "Where's Popkin?" asked the rabbi. "He's got to get..." He stopped after hearing the sound of horses. Within seconds, a large wagon with the printed words POPKIN'S FURNITURE pulled into view. A number of men scurried to the wagon, unloaded the empty, crudely and quickly constructed plain wooden caskets and placed them into the freshly dug graves. The men quickly refilled the holes with dirt and the rabbi placed makeshift wooden crosses at the heads of each plot. He wanted to hug the men who helped, but simply nodded and they all vanished as quickly as they had appeared. Now, it became a waiting game for the rabbi. He stood alone in the spot where he discovered the three women and one badly wounded man. He was a preacher at heart, but realized he'd have to perform magic using empty boxes as props.

Looking skyward, the rabbi said a prayer. Despite the overwhelming seriousness of his predicament, he chuckled to himself. Who, other than God, could have predicted that when he woke up this morning he'd be standing sentry over four fake graves with handmade crosses constructed by his own hands?

He thought about a passage in Proverbs: *The Lord works out everything to its proper end— even the wicked for a day of disaster.* The lives of four human beings rested in his hands. Rabbi Solomon didn't ask for this mission. It was God's will, and he was fully prepared to accept the responsibility. He'd dealt with outlaws in the past, some more onerous than others. They all had something in common, a lack of upbringing and faith. Rabbi

Solomon didn't blame anyone. A wise man knows that a person's behaviors are rooted from his or her upbringing. Who knew what possessed these two outlaws, the brothers Bailey, to kill and hunt humans like they were so much meat. He felt a tinge of sadness. It wasn't what God had planned for them, he was certain of that. And he knew that all souls on earth could be rehabilitated if given the chance. Why not? He'd gone astray as a young man. He was open about it to his small congregation. His frankness and honesty had given him credibility amongst his congregation. He thought about poor Clem Stallings, the innocent victim of a gunshot wound. How many thoughtless and wasteful killings had he seen over the years? Too many. As he waited, he prayed again for the full recovery of Clem Stallings. He pulled a small worn leather book from the back pocket of his trousers and read. He didn't hear the two men on horseback who approached.

Jed Bailey interrupted the rabbi. "Hey, you with the beard. Look up at me," he commanded.

Startled, Rabbi Solomon replaced the book in his back pocket and stared at the man speaking.

"You see four people come through here?" asked Jed.

Rabbi Solomon sized up the pair. They were filthy and looked tired, desperate, and dangerous. "Do you need food and water, my friends?" asked Solomon.

Jed looked at brother Pit and spat. "That's not what I asked you, now is it? One more time, mister, and if I don't like the answer from you... well, it's going to be too bad for you. Have you seen four people—three women and a man? The man might be injured."

Rabbi Solomon lowered his eyes. He spread his hands, as if showing a prized horse. "If you are referring to the four strangers we have buried here, then yes. There were three women and one injured man. I came across them when—"

"Shuddup, old-timer!" Jed Bailey surveyed the scene, taking in the fresh graves and crosses. "You buried four people?"

"That's exactly what I'm saying," responded Solomon.

Pit Bailey sneered. "I don't believe him, Jed. Look at him. Long beard, funny things hanging out of his shirt, I tell ya, I don't like the looks a him. Why you dressed like that, old man?"

"What's wrong with my dress?" Solomon figured the longer he kept the conversation away from the four people in hiding the better. "This is how I dress."

"What are you, some kind of a monk or something?" asked Pit. "I ain't never seen nobody look like you."

"I assure you this is normal dress," answered Solomon. "I am a rabbi."

"A what?" asked the brothers in unison.

"A rabbi. I am a scholar, a teacher. I'm considered a religious leader of the Jewish people in these parts. We are few in number but a proud people. Are you sure I can't get you some drink and food? You look awfully thirsty and hungry. I have water back there where you can wash up a bit."

"This crazy man gives me a headache," said Pit. "I think he's hiding them women and that piano man. I bet he knows where they are. Hell, they couldn't be far from here."

Jed Bailey swiveled his head looking for any signs of the four. "I don't know, Pit. What 'bout them graves right here? What 'bout them?"

"I say we dig 'em up and see fer ourselves. That's what I say. And if we find this here old fool is lying to us... well, we won't have to dig him a grave, now will we? We got us four different ones we can choose from." Hyena-like laughter followed. "Whaddya say, old man? You got you a shovel so we can start digging and see for ourselves?"

Rabbi Solomon stood firm. He wasn't a gambling man; he knew about its sin and what it could do to a person. But he calculated the odds against outsmarting this duo and figured they were in his favor. "Brains outsmart brawn," his father used to say. He repeated the three words to himself over and over. "I do, back in the house. I can get it for you, but digging up a grave is blasphemous."

The brothers looked at each other and then stared back at Rabbi Solomon. Neither man spoke for several seconds and then Pit broke the silence. "Hell, we don't need no shovel. We'll dig 'em up with our hands. You better hope we find four bodies in these graves, Mr. Big Mouth with a beard. Let's go, Jed."

The brothers jumped off their horses and stared down at one of the graves. "What you are about to do is a sin, gentlemen," warned the rabbi. "But if that is your choice, you'll face God and the consequences. You won't have to worry about me." The rabbi took a few steps back.

Pit got down on his knees and started tossing dirt with his bare hands. He repeatedly heaved dual palms-full over his shoulder. Jed, hesitant, watched. Pit said, "What's the matter with you, Jed? You ain't worried 'bout what he says, are ya? Git down here and help me. The quicker we find out if he's lying, the quicker we find them four who can identify us."

Reluctantly, Jed bent his knees and began heaving piles of dirt as well. Rabbi Solomon stood watching, thinking. He pulled the small leather volume from his pocket, opened it and began reading. The words were in Hebrew. He whispered, his voice barely audible to the Bailey brothers. He kept one eye on the page and one on the two diggers. They were making progress. Rabbi Solomon began chanting the words a little louder.

"Keep going, Jed," ordered Pit. "I'll be damned if we're gonna come across a dead man's box. I'll wager anything this old coot is lying through that beard of his. Let's give it another few... Wait, what's this? Dig faster! I think I felt something hard. I... faster." The brothers somehow summoned up the energy and increased their digging speed. "Well, I'll be damned," said Pit. "Will ya look at that! A wooden box. Maybe this old blabbering fool was tellin' us the truth, Jed. Whaddya think? We dig up the other piles and make sure they got boxes in them as well?"

The rabbi continued reading, pretending to ignore the brothers. He didn't like what he heard next out of Jed's filthy mouth.

"I don't know, Pit. Just 'cause there's a box in the ground don't mean it got a body in it. Or even if it does, it don't mean it's one of them dance hall women or that piano playin' man. I say we take us a look inside this box and see for ourselves."

The rabbi's chant became louder. With rapidity, he bowed back and forth, as he changed pitch in his voice, emphasizing certain words and phrases.

"Will you shut up, old man!" screamed Pit. "I'm tryin' to think."

The rabbi's voice became louder, almost robotic in his dialect. He lowered the book. "I'm reading scripture."

"What?" asked Pit.

"Scripture. God's words."

"What's God saying, old man?" Jed asked, laughter in his voice.

"God's words are in Leviticus. *Nor shall he approach any dead person.* And if I'm not mistaken, the Lord's words in Ezekiel say, *They shall not go to a dead person to defile themselves...*"

"That's nothin' but mumbo jumbo," said Jed.

"Are you gambling men?" asked Rabbi Solomon. "Are you willing to risk the word of God for the sake of defiling yourselves? It is up to you. You see the graves. You have witnessed a casket. Haven't you seen enough? I assure you there are three additional caskets buried under these dirt piles. You risk eternal punishment for upsetting a grave. Think about it, gentlemen. You have eyes. You see the casket. For your own sakes, let the dead rest in peace." The rabbi continued reading Hebrew words aloud.

Jed was ready to ignore Solomon and open the casket, but Pit, displaying a rare modicum of sense and restraint, had doubts. "Hold on there, Jed. You heard the man. Eternal punishment."

"Eternal *damnation*," chimed Solomon.

"Are you gonna believe this old fool and his foolish talk? How much worse could it be fer us anyway? We already done our share of killings and stealings. This ain't nothin' more than that," said Jed.

Pit scratched his chin. "I don't know. I ain't so sure 'bout it is all. I mean, sure, we done killed. But we ain't never messed with no dead bodies. There's just something 'bout it..."

Jed looked disgusted. "Oh, then jest forget 'bout it. They ain't gonna identify us from under the ground. Let's just head on back."

Pit stared down Rabbi Solomon. "You better be tellin' us the truth, old man. That's all I can say fer you."

Rabbi Solomon smiled and bowed. He watched the two outlaws mount their horses and ride away. He looked skyward. "Thank you," he said.

*****

A little less than three months later, Beverly, Sally, and Jane sat at the kitchen table and after finishing their eggs and bread breakfast, sipped coffee. Beverly turned to the rabbi's wife, Sarah Solomon. "Why do you do this for us? Share your home? Your food?" The three women stared at Sarah.

The petite woman wiped her hands on a towel. "We follow God's commandments. Isaiah says, *to share your bread with the hungry.* When your friend is up and about and you feel safe to travel, you will again be on your own. Until then, we are happy to help. We believe in and practice Tikkun Olam. That means repairing the world through acts of kindness."

A jubilant Rabbi Solomon interrupted them. "I have wonderful news!" he shouted, slamming the door behind him. "I've—"

Sarah stopped him. "Are you not going to say 'Good morning' to our guests?" she asked.

The rabbi stopped in his tracks. Embarrassed, he quickly recovered. "Yes... yes, of course. Good morning, everyone." With that out of the way, he blurted out, "Your friend Clem Stallings is well. The doctor says he's ready to travel. Our prayers have been answered!"

The moment, bittersweet, brought everyone to tears. "We'll miss you all," said Sarah.

"Yes," agreed Rabbi Solomon, nodding. "But St. Louis is a wonderful place. You will all have new lives and new futures, and with God's blessing it will be free of violence. You'll find plenty of singing opportunities and dancing opportunities in respectable dance halls. I've been there myself. I know!" He chuckled. "And Mr. Stallings' gifted fingers will again play beautiful music. If I were a betting man," he momentarily paused, "I'd bet you four have pretty good futures ahead of you."

After a moment of awkward silence, Rabbi Solomon walked over to a cabinet and removed three leather books. He handed each woman one. "I already gave Clem his copy."

"A Bible?" asked Jane Taylor.

"Yes," answered the rabbi.

Sally Newsome cleared her throat. "That's very nice, Rabbi Solomon. You know there is no way we could ever thank you or repay you and Sarah for your kindness and food and shelter and love and everything else."

"Ah, but you can pay me back," said the rabbi.

Beverly spoke. "How's that? We aren't Jews." She held up the book. "This will not make us Jewish."

"No, indeed not. It is not my place to proselytize. You believe or do not believe as you see fit and whatever makes you comfortable. I ask only one thing as payment."

"Yes?" they said in unison.

Remember God's words in Deuteronomy: *You shall open wide your hand to your brother, to the needy and to the poor, in your land.*

*****

"Well, will you look at this," said Clem Stallings, pointing a finger at a folded newspaper. He sat on a piano bench an hour prior to starting time.

"What?" asked Beverly Diamante. She had dropped the 'Diamond' name after establishing herself in St. Louis.

Stallings read, "In a double hanging, brothers Jed and Pit Bailey met their Maker for the murderous attack at the Grizzly Creek saloon. Dubbed by the press at the time 'Grizzly Creek Runs Red,' the brothers were captured and brought to trial a year to the day after their rampage."

"Anything else?" asked Beverly.

Clem scanned the article. "Says here the two outlaws were identified by a nameless man whose only public statement quoted Leviticus: *Anyone who takes the life of a human being is to be put to death.*"

The End

Scott Harris

Brothers' Love

By

Justin Harris

A peaceful rain danced on the roof the last time Grant saw Sarah. The fire was crackling, and they had spent the evening reading the Bible together, eating, and laughing. He could still smell the pine smoke mixing with the fragrance of her hair and could still taste the elk steak she had fried up. Sarah had said she didn't trust Grant and his brothers to avoid trouble, so Grant had opened up to the book of Psalms and reminded her that it was "better to put trust in the Lord than to put confidence in a man."

The trail is a dangerous place to get lost in one's thoughts, and though he knew better, he couldn't stop thinking about how her hair and the fresh rain and the fire combined to make the most perfect and enticing smell. His brother Dustin jolted him back to reality.

"Keep a sharp eye out ahead. This turn provides perfect cover."

Most of the ground they had covered on this trail was out in the plains of the high desert, providing little to no cover. This suited them just fine, as it also provided no cover for bandits. But as the trail wound through this small canyon, they lost all the protection of flat, open ground.

The treasure they were carrying was insignificant compared to what most bandits were looking for on these trails. The five brothers weren't carrying the pay for a mining outfit, or a large load for a bank, but carrying their own small family fortune. The brothers had spent the winter hunting buffalo and were returning with a wagonful of thick—and valuable—winter coats. They were traveling from Wyoming to the Colorado Territory, preparing to start a new, stable life together. And while the cargo may have been less than bandits were ideally looking for, it was certainly a cargo they'd be willing to accept.

The brothers hoped that five armed men, with only a single wagon to protect, would dissuade smaller, weaker gangs, while the smarter large gangs that could read the risks and rewards would determine that five armed men was too much work for a single wagonload of hides. That logic made sense from the safety of a home or a hotel, but logic rarely plays out on the trail.

"Jeremy, head up front with Dustin. I've got the rear. Tom, get the scattergun ready. Jarrod, the horses need to be ready to fly. If we come 'round the bend and there's a gang waiting, we're pushing hard and through them. If a trap is set, I'll keep our backside covered, and you don't stop pushing this wagon until we're clean through the canyon."

Despite being the youngest and the most given to daydreaming, Grant was the best with a gun, and the best at avoiding using a gun. He had spent years tracking, scouting, shooting, and fighting; and his talent at each was unquestioned. All the brothers had served in the War Between the States, but Grant had stayed on the trail almost continuously since then.

He knew that Dustin and Jeremy were the best horsemen and unafraid to ride headlong into trouble. Tom was the biggest and strongest, and could handle a scattergun on a bouncy wagon ride. Jarrod was able to keep cool in tough situations, stick to plans, and think on his feet, and there was no one he would rather have driving the wagon. Grant felt as prepared as he could be, with his brothers positioned the best possible way for success.

As they turned the corner, an eerie silence fell over them, like the battle they were expecting just wasn't there. They pushed along at a good clip, but slowly enough to evaluate the surroundings. Jeremy's shoulders finally relaxed up front and he turned to Dustin, saying, "I told you there was nothing to worry about."

Dustin laughed a little and started to relax as well. He turned back to yell at Jarrod and Tom, just in time to see Grant lift his rifle and snap off two quick shots. The four older brothers heard horses thundering off in the other direction, unsure of what had happened and what was about to happen.

"Keep pushing!" Grant yelled, knowing his brothers would be unsure how to react to a single-pronged attack where only he faced danger. But the attack was too weak to be a genuine attempt. Grant was confident that the purpose of the rear attack was to get them to stop where they could be pinned, and possibly to distract them or have their guns facing the wrong way.

Pushing forward felt wrong—it felt like leaving one brother behind—but pushing was what they agreed to do and what Grant was calling for them to do, so push they did. Jeremy and Dustin never had trouble riding headlong into trouble, but it felt to them as though they were riding headlong away from trouble and leaving their little brother to fend for himself.

Five or six sharp snaps eased all worry about running from trouble. There was a rock outcropping west of the trail, and whoever was behind it had a perfect bead on them. Jeremy took a round to the shoulder but galloped on ahead, returning fire with a Smith & Wesson Model 3. With Dustin now riding between Jeremy and the wagon, it became clear that there were at least three more bandits waiting behind the rock; one concentrating on the wagon, one on Dustin and one on Jeremy.

Tom had begun to return fire with the scattergun, giving Jeremy and Dustin momentary reprieve. Jeremy was coming close to flanking them on his mad dash, but the rock outcropping stayed silent even after Tom stopped firing.

Had they not continued pushing and gone to help Grant on the rear attack, the rocks would have provided perfect cover and they would have been trapped in deadly crossfire. As it stood now, Jeremy's bold ride was threatening to outflank them. Given how easily both ends of the attacks had been foiled, the bandits decided to saddle up and ride off before they could be caught up in the type of crossfire they had planned on delivering themselves.

Jeremy began to give chase, snapping off the last two rounds in his pistol.

"Jeremy, get back here! Let's stay together!" Dustin shouted.

Outflanking a position that was firing on them was one thing. Chasing multiple men with an empty gun and leaving your wagon behind with a bullet in your shoulder was another thing altogether. Jeremy turned and rode back, and all of them regrouped at the wagon.

"We're still a day and a half of hard riding out of Denver, and we need to get there before Jeremy loses what's left of his arm," Tom said, looking down from the wagon at the bloody mess hanging from Jeremy's shoulder.

"Are we out of the woods on this trail yet?" Dustin asked.

"I think we're safe for now, but I can't comment on the next forty or so miles. But once we leave this canyon, we're back on flat open ground and should be fine," Grant responded.

"So, what do we do from here?" Tom asked.

"We need to clean and dress Jeremy's shoulder. Then let's put him on the wagon with Jarrod. We'll make the best time that we can and try to get him to the doc before anything too permanent sets in. And we'll just have to stay vigilant for the rest of the trail; they may be coming back to finish what they started," Dustin stated.

"I don't think they're regrouping or coming back. They didn't lose any men in the rocks and still fled. Far as I can tell, they only lost one of the two men in the rear. They saw a single wagon and a few men and thought they found a soft target. When it turned out we fought back, they hightailed. They're looking for easy targets, not trying to double up on hard targets," Grant responded. "Tom, get some water boiling and grab some whiskey. Dustin, cut Jeremy's sleeve off. Let's see how bad this arm is. And someone go grab Jarrod. Why is he still just sitting up on that wagon?"

Tom grabbed the bottle of whiskey from the back of the wagon but almost immediately, it fell and shattered. The sound of glass exploding tore through the air, and Grant, Dustin and Jeremy looked over.

"Jarrod was hit!" Tom yelled as he jumped up on the wagon, grabbing Jarrod's limp body and laying him across the bench. He frantically cut away the blood-stained shirt as it seemed to fight his every movement, clinging to Jarrod's chest. Pants were manically ripped away. Two holes were immediately revealed—one dead center on the right breast, and one clear through his thigh.

There was no breath left in Jarrod's lungs and no way to revive him. The blood loss from either shot probably would have been enough to kill him, but combined, he stood no chance. The four brothers collectively dropped their heads for what seemed like eternity, each saying a prayer for their departed brother and saying another prayer for each other.

After a few moments of silence, Grant spoke up. "Well, boys, we need to get moving. Got to get across the Grizzly before nightfall or we're gonna be sitting ducks here tonight. Let's put Jarrod in the wagon with the pelts—most comfortable ride he'll ever have—and get him back to civilization. Have a proper funeral with the family, not bury him out here on some Godforsaken trail."

The brothers began moving in a trance-like state. Jarrod was loaded in the back of the wagon, while Tom and Dustin tended to Jeremy. Grant grabbed and reloaded all the weapons they had to make sure they would be ready for any further action. He also went around the back of the wagon and retrieved the four .50-90 Sharps rifles they had used to take down the buffalo. Grant assumed that these would be virtually useless on the trail if they were attacked again, which is why they were weren't loaded and out in the first place, but he also knew that now was not the time to be making assumptions.

With everything packed and ready to go, yet still moving in silence as though guided by a siren that only they could hear, the four brothers mounted back up and prepared to ride the trail. But before they started their ride, Grant asked his brothers to remove their hats and bow their heads.

"Lord, I don't know what your plan is, but I know you will guide us through this. I can't comprehend your will or why you would take such a loyal and faithful servant, but I ask that you guide us safely home through the rest of this journey. Despite a violent enemy stalking us, I find comfort in your word. Today, we walk through the valley of the shadow of death, yet we will fear no evil; for you are with us. Your rod and your staff comfort us. With your blessing, powerful and merciful Lord, we will complete our journey with our lives and our bodies intact. Amen."

The gun battle, the loss of their brother, the injury to Jeremy, and the unanticipated time standing around in the heat had exhausted all of them. But unlike the remaining four Heid brothers, the hours lacked the emotional investment in the loss of a brother to spur them on, and their exhaustion was beginning to show.

"If we keep pushing, we can get to the Grizzly in about an hour, let the horses drink up, cross over, and set up a camp where we can defend ourselves," Grant said to no one in particular. There wasn't really another option. There was no water between them and the Grizzly, and the horses needed water. And trying to make some sort of camp in this open, flat, coverless patch of plains would be foolish.

Unable to sit in silence any longer, Tom asked the uncomfortable question on everyone's mind. "Once we make it to Denver, how do we ensure we get justice for Jarrod?"

Jeremy said, "We'll talk to the marshal. Let him know what happened. I'm sure he'll have a clue who this gang is. And if the marshal can't or won't handle this, then we'll ride back out and handle it ourselves. Well, maybe you three will have to handle it. I might be laying up in a hospital bed, talking about how I used to have two arms."

"Right now, the focus has to be getting to Denver without catching any more bullets, and that starts with getting across the Grizzly and finding some cover." Dustin looked back from his horse, locking eyes with Jeremy. "But trust me, brother, you'll be ready. And if you have to come out here with only one arm, you'll be riding with us as we exact the debt we are owed from those cowards."

The four of them rode along in silence, pondering what was to come in the immediate future, and how they were going to deal with this tragedy long term. Finally the monotony of the plains was broken by the sight of trees and green grass, and ever so faintly they could hear the Grizzly running in the distance.

Grizzly Creek is an inherently peaceful place. A mini-oasis, with lush grass and large trees snaking along its banks, offering a break from the high desert plains. The east side of the creek is flat and almost barren, but the west side abutts two beautiful rolling hills. Atop the hills on either side of the crossing sit large rock outcroppings, large enough to provide shelter and cover, and with enough of a view of the surrounding plains to ensure approaches can be seen from all sides.

As the creek and the hills came into view, the four brothers could envision getting camp set up and having a night of relative peace, as they would begin to process what they had gone through that day. The silence, only punctuated by the ever-flowing water, seemed to invite them to be calm and relaxed, as though they had made it home. They were still a good ten minutes from hitting the creek when the caravan was brought to a sudden halt.

"Hold up here for a minute. Something isn't right," Grant said as he dismounted.

He reached down to the ground and grabbed some blades of grass, furiously rubbing them between his hands and taking a deep breath of the fresh fragrance. He picked up some dirt, gently dropping it in front of his own face, watching how the wind carried it down. He then lay with his ears to the ground, listening for any signs of trouble.

"What are you doing down there, rolling in the dirt? Let's get over and across this creek and set up. I don't like sitting out here in the open, and my shoulder is killing me."

"Can you just be quiet and listen for minute, or at least be quiet and let me?" Grant shot back.

"Listen for what? All I hear is that damn creek, and sitting here for an hour won't change that."

"Jeremy, only you can be so wrong that you're actually right. Yes, you can't hear anything other than a creek, but isn't that odd? We're out here near the only water source around, and I don't hear or see any animals. This much silence in a place that should be drawing all the local animals means that something has spooked them. Some sort of predator. And my best guess, when it's this silent for this long, is that the predator can only be humans."

"Well, if they're waiting for us, we're heading straight into a trap. Already been in one of those today, and I don't really fancy heading straight into another one. On the other hand, it might just be quiet, and we will need to get across that eventually. How do we figure out for sure?" Tom asked.

Dustin looked over his brothers, took a deep breath and explained the situation as best he saw it. "Even if it is a trap, what other option do we have? The horses are burnt out and in need of water, we're about out of food, and I'm sick of running from some cowards that already shot two of my brothers. Plus, heading back over the plains won't do anything but make us sitting ducks when they come back tomorrow, and we don't even know that they are waiting for us."

"Well, let's at least try to maximize the small tree cover on this side. We'll ride up—not close enough to be in range, but close enough to reach those couple of birch trees. Tom and I will get behind the trees with the buffalo guns to provide cover. Dustin, you're the best rider left. Well, at least you're the best of the riders with two working arms. You head out and cross the creek as fast as you can, and Tom and I will cover you with the Sharps. If they fire, you make it back here while we provide cover, and we'll prepare to go from there. If you make it across without receiving fire, head straight up the closest hill and take the high ground. Then we'll cross with you providing cover for us. But be aware going up that hill, there's a chance they let you cross to not give away their position, and bait us into bringing these buffalo hides down into their trap."

"I can't abide that," Jeremy announced defiantly. "I may be down a wing, but I can still ride, and no point in risking a third brother getting shot today. I'll be riding point, and those of you with two arms can provide the cover."

With a plan set, the brothers took a few minutes to ready themselves before they bowed their heads once more. This time, Jeremy led them in a quick prayer.

"Lord, us Heid brothers are but your humble servants. We seek to glorify you in all that we do, and we are so thankful for the blessings you have bestowed upon us. We humbly ask for your protection and grace as we attempt to cross this creek. In Jesus's name, we pray. Amen."

Tom and Grant picked up their Sharps and began to walk to the trees. Dustin and Jeremy were busy checking that everything was locked and loaded, as Dustin begged Jeremy to let him ride. "You're down an arm and a ton of blood. You shouldn't be the one heading out on this crossing."

"Whoever leads this crossing is gonna be worthless with a gun. Can't shoot up into those mountains with a pistol, and that's one gun down. If you go, we're two guns down with my arm. Just have that Winchester out and ready, and be mounted and ready to ride. I'll see you on the other side, older brother."

Dustin helped Jeremy onto his mount and watched as he struggled to control the reins with one hand. He then mounted up his horse and watched as his brother rode off. For the second time today, Dustin felt like he was abandoning a brother in the middle of a firefight, and it wasn't a feeling he thought he could ever get used to. He had his eyes peeled, looking for any sign of trouble—the glint of the sun off a barrel, sound or movement giving away a location—just looking for anywhere he could aim his rifle to feel less helpless.

Jeremy approached the water slowly and cautiously, with his eyes and ears straining to find any danger. As the first hoof hit the water, the splash seemed to echo for days, as though calling in danger from anywhere within earshot. The creek was relatively shallow, about eighteen inches deep in the middle, not deep enough to cause much trouble for a horse, especially one that he had trained so well to deal with water. But he was having to fight the horse with his only good hand, as the tired and exhausted animal wanted nothing more than to stick its head down in the cool, clear water and drink its fill.

Leaning down on the horse's neck, Jeremy whispered, "I know you're thirsty, but just get us to the other side of this creek, and once they are all across you can drink, roll around and eat all of the beautiful grass on the banks. We're almost through this, boy."

Suddenly, the silence was broken by three shots fired in rapid succession. Jeremy immediately yanked on the reins to turn the horse around, but two more shots rang out and horse and rider were downed instantaneously. The clear, cool water immediately ran red.

Tom and Grant saw the shots coming from a rock outcropping atop the hill and immediately returned fire, causing the men to duck back down into their well-fortified positions. Yet before the first volley was over, they saw Dustin galloping full speed past them, heading out to Jeremy in the creek.

Grant picked up his Winchester to save the ammo on the two remaining Sharps that were loaded, and began firing at the rocks, hoping to provide enough cover for Dustin. The men were well fortified, sitting in the middle of the rocks behind a large boulder, providing virtually unlimited cover.

"We can't flush them from here. They have perfect cover. Take the buffalo rifles and shoot above them. See if some rocks falling on them can't flush them out!" Grant yelled to Tom, as he continued to provide cover fire.

Dustin reached the creek and immediately jumped down off his horse. He pulled Jeremy out from under the downed horse and immediately threw him up over his own saddle. He then jumped back on the horse with Jeremy behind him, and instead of turning back towards Tom and Grant, he charged forward full speed ahead. Crossing the creek at a gallop, he immediately began heading up the hill towards the bandits, with Jeremy barely able to sit with a now damaged leg and his shot-up arm, somehow holding a pistol and ready to fire.

Tom grabbed the two loaded Sharps and fired two quick shots to the rocks above the bandits' heads that sent a large boulder straight down while smaller debris flew everywhere. Four men scattered like cockroaches. Two bandits ran farther up the hill, and two ran down the path towards the creek.

Grant picked off the first of the four with a gut shot as soon as he left the cover of the boulder. The man behind him jumped over the fallen man as he raced for the next boulder that could provide cover. But before he could reach safety, a round from Grant's Winchester exploded through the back of his knee, leaving both men bleeding and yelling in pain.

Heading down the trail, the other two men were unprepared for Dustin and Jeremy, who were charging up the trail at full speed. Before they could even take aim, Dustin put a bullet through the first one's neck and Jeremy winged the second man. Dustin didn't slow down as the two men stood there, stunned and shot up. The first man fell, gurgling on his own blood and barely missed being trampled as he fell off the trail and rolled down the hill. The second man, who had dropped his weapon after being winged, lacked the reflexes to avoid the two thousand pounds of angry horse and man, and was leveled and trampled.

Tom and Grant mounted up and chased their brothers as fast as the horses would carry. And with only a single rider on each horse, they were making up ground quickly. Dustin and Jeremy arrived at the place where the bandits had been taking cover, only to find the trail blocked by a boulder with a fifth bandit flattened underneath it. As Dustin tried to figure out a way around the boulder, Tom and Grant came galloping up him.

"Let's stay behind this boulder. I don't want anyone jumping right into a final trap," Tom said as he pulled Dustin back.

Grant yelled, "Now I know both you men are shot, you've lost another three men here at the creek, and at least one more earlier today. You ain't got no right to live, but if you surrender now, we'll ensure you're taken alive to hospital in Denver. If not, you'll simply be added to today's deaths."

"Ah, hell, surrender? I can't even move. I'm shot in my gut, and you just about shot his leg off. Just get us a damn doctor."

"We're heading around this boulder, and this is your only shot. Anything other than complete surrender will mean a slow and painful death. But a complete surrender means a doctor." With that, Grant climbed the boulder, jumped down the other side, and found both men in a lot of pain but very much alive. He quickly kicked their weapons out of reach and called over his brothers.

"We're all clear over here. Grab some rope. Let's tie these men up."

Dustin, rage and energy still coursing through his veins, grabbed Grant by the chest, pulling him away from the bandits as Tom tied them up. "Why would we allow these cowards to live? They shot Jeremy, they killed Jarrod, and they tried to rob us twice. They deserve to die!"

"And die they will, at the end of rope. But I don't care about what they deserve. Our parents deserve to be there when it happens. Plus, a bullet now would be a gift. Let them suffer through the wounds and suffer in jail. And then let's watch them dance when their feet don't even touch the ground."

Before the brothers made camp or took care of their horses, they went over to check on Jeremy, fearing the worst.

"No need to stress over me, boys. Horse shot out from under me—he fell on me and with my busted arm I couldn't get free. Luckily Dustin had the courage to ride out there, while you boys were playing in the trees."

Despite (or maybe because of) all the tragedy of the day, Jeremy's playful barb elicited much more laughter than it deserved. The four of them sat down for a minute, attempting to catch their breath and calm down. The sun was beginning to set, and the sky was instantly transformed by a combination of reds and oranges, while the creek below them ran a deep crimson with the blood of a fallen horse.

"Well, boys, I guess we need to make camp and take care of the horses. Let's leave the dead bandits where they are. Cowards like that deserve only to be discovered by buzzards. Tomorrow we still need to finish this journey, and we'll have to transport two wounded prisoners," Dustin proclaimed.

Despite making camp, rest was almost impossible to come by. The sadness of what had happened, the realization of what they were still facing, the idea of telling their parents, were all weighing on their minds. They had no food, beyond the last couple hard biscuits, and the constant moaning of their two prisoners ensured that it wasn't just their emotions keeping them from getting any rest.

And yet, about ten yards away from camp, Grant lay peacefully with his eyes closed tightly.

Once again, he could smell the pine, hear the rain, feel the fire, and taste the elk steaks, but most importantly, he could see, hear, and smell Sarah. The trail may be a dangerous place to get lost in one's thoughts, but sometimes getting lost in one's own thoughts is the only way to deal with the tragedies of the trail.

The Last Trap

by

Scott Harris

It strikes me as odd that at only twenty years of age, I'm working in a business, an industry, that is slowly dying. But it is 1842 and beaver trapping isn't nearly as easy or as lucrative as it was for the men who came before me. Old timers, like Joe Meek, tell stories about being able to catch all the beaver you wanted and about times when you were only limited by how many pelts you could pack out.

Looking around the campground at the three men I'm traveling with, I realize all of them have been doing this far longer than the four years I've been trapping, and one of them, Oregon Bill, has been doing it longer than I've been alive. All of them remember days when it was easier—and safer.

Sure, we still have to deal with the things that all Oregon trappers have always dealt with: insects, terrible weather, disease, injury, hostile Indians, and the one that scares me the most— grizzly bears. Even after four years of doing this, they're still pretty much the last thing I think about every night before I fall asleep and the first thing that crosses my mind when I hear a strange sound.

I don't suppose I'll ever get the image of Big Jim, torn to shreds and spread out over his camp, out of my head. I think back to when he taught me to trap and how huge he was. How he lived without fear. I always figured nobody, or nothing, could ever kill Big Jim. But there he was, spread out all over his camp, those giant grizzly tracks making it obvious what happened. The three days it took me to track down that grizz and kill 'im were the worst of my life. All I could think about was what had happened to Jim and how, if it happened to him, it could easily happen to me.

I musta gotten lost in my thoughts, 'cause I can hear Mississippi asking, "Dusty? Dusty, you with us?"

I look up and smile, answering, "Yeah. Just thinking about not trapping anymore. Only a couple of days left before we get to Fort

Vancouver, and once we sell these off to the Hudson Bay Company, I think I'm gonna be done."

"You thinkin' about going from being a free trader to a company man, working for Hudson?"

"No. I mean done. Trapped my last beaver." As I listen to myself, I'm surprised by the decisiveness of my answer. I guess I really am done.

"Whatcha gonna do instead?"

"Don't know. Just figure it's getting too dangerous out here, especially since the outlaws have decided it's easier to wait till we're on our way to the fort and rob us, instead of doing any work themselves. I'm okay with fighting the elements, the Indians and even the grizzlies, but I don't want any part of having to fight outlaws that last hundred miles every year.

"The days of beaver pelts being 'soft gold' seem like they're behind us. I can't see ever wearing anything but a beaver hat, but people seem to like those new silk hats I keep hearing about. Just ain't the money in it anymore since you old men took all the easy beaver, and I don't figure on staying out here until I get et by a grizzly or shot, soft gold or not."

They all laughed easily and took sips from their coffee.

Oregon Bill, who'd been trapping for more than thirty years and was alone for more than half of it, usually didn't say much, but he spoke up.

"I've been thinkin' about it for the last couple of weeks, since before we met up. I've got some money down in a bank in San Francisco. Been going there every year or two for a long time and have a bit saved up."

I had no idea Bill ever left Oregon, and when I looked at Mississippi and Pelt Pete, it's clear they didn't either. Even rarer than Bill speaking is him smiling, but he does now, knowing he's surprised us.

"I even had a girl there for a couple of years. Might want to find her again. Anyway, I'm thinkin' when we sell these off"—he points to a very large supply of beaver pelts that we'd collected over the previous few months—"I'll have enough money to buy me a little place. Run a couple of cattle, just enough so I don't have to ever hunt again, but I'll make sure it's alongside a creek, so I can do some fishing, maybe watch the beavers build a dam. Never watched 'em work before, but I think I might enjoy it."

Mississippi and Pelt Pete seem as surprised as I am that Bill is going to be done. He's been doing it for so long that I guess none of us ever thought he'd stop.

Pete looks up from his coffee, laughs and says, "Me? I think I've got another couple of seasons left. Don't know much else, and maybe I can save a little money too. Maybe get a cabin next to yours,

Bill. Sounds nice. Plus, I'd like to meet the girl that wants to live with you in a cabin."

Even Bill laughs at that.

Pete keeps going. "You staying, 'Sippi? With all these outlaws showing up, don't think I want to trap alone no more."

Mississippi pours himself another cup of hot coffee, the steam rising from his cup and disappearing into the branches of the big white oak tree he's leaning against.

I pour myself another cup as well, as much for defense against the growing cold as for the taste.

Mississippi answers Pete. "Sure, I'll stay. I only know cards and beaver, and I never was any good at cards. I mighta been the only professional gambler on the Mississippi River circuit where people hoped I played in their games. Trappin's gettin' tougher, but it still beats anything else I can think of. Yeah, I'll go another season or two with ya, Pete."

After that, the conversation just kinda dies out. I guess we all have plenty to think about. It's my turn to clean up, so I walk the pots down to the creek and clean 'em out. Then I roll myself a cigarette and settle in for a few minutes. It's cold, but the trees block the wind, and I like the sound of the creek when there are no other sounds. Feels like rain's coming, but maybe we'll make it back to the fort before it hits.

It's been a good few years, trapping beaver. I enjoy the time alone, and I've had a spell of good luck—never getting sick or hurt—and managed to never run into any hostile Indians. But, as much as I enjoy the months alone, it has been fun to meet up with Oregon Bill, Mississippi and Pelt Pete for the last one hundred miles to the fort. Feels a lot safer. I think I'll miss this part the most.

The cigarette done, I walk back to camp and find Bill and Pete already sound asleep.

Mississippi is on guard duty and whispers to be sure it's me coming back. I answer quietly, throw a few more sticks on the fire and settle in, thankful that tonight it's my turn to not have to take a shift.

*****

Pete wakes us at dawn. It's nice to see the fire already going and the coffee boiling. The man who skips watch has to get the three pack mules ready, so I crawl outta my bedroll and get to work. I like working with the mules, and I like sleeping through the night, so these are my favorite mornings. As the man who took the last shift, Pete's only job is to get the fire and the coffee going, and since that's done, he sits back and watches as Mississippi and Bill get breakfast cooking.

Bill has a magical way with biscuits, and I'm pleased to see he's working on some now. I think the secret is the amount of salt, but he won't say and says he never will. I can see he's using up the end of the fixin's—there's maybe enough for another day—so I'm glad we're close to the fort. Mississippi is boiling up the last of the elk steaks. But we either gotta do a little more hunting between here and the fort or tighten our belts that last day or so. I do enjoy a good elk steak, but by the end of the season, I'm usually pretty happy to see something else. This year's no different, and I let my mind wander to Fort Vancouver, where the first thing I'm going to do is get some fresh scrambled eggs and a big glass of ice cold milk.

None of us are what you would call enthusiastic about mornings, though we all do our part without complaint. However, conversation is at a minimum, and grunts, pointing and habit are pretty much all we need to get ready to ride. As we sit our horses, taking one last look around at our site, we might not have said ten words all morning, which is fine with each of us, especially Bill.

*****

After riding about five hours, we stop for our midday meal. It's my turn to backtrail a bit and make sure we're not being followed by unwelcome guests, and Bill rides ahead to ensure we don't ride into something we don't want to. Pete and Mississippi take care of their horses, the three mules and putting something together to eat, which pretty much means the end of the biscuits.

I ride back about two miles, stopping just short of cresting the last hill we rode over before we stopped. I tie off my horse and work my way to the top, keeping my head low and my movements slow. I take off my hat and use it to shade my eyes from the sun, which, while not doing much to heat things up, is still bright.

I watch for about five minutes, feeling good that I haven't seen anything out of the ordinary and that the large bear I do see is moving away from us. Just as I'm starting to stand up, a movement off in the distance catches my eye. I watch for a couple of minutes until it becomes clear it's riders. Eight of them. They don't have any pack mules or horses, and they don't seem to be carrying a lot of gear. Both those things make me nervous, and my stomach instantly starts to churn, just a little.

There's not much out here besides Indians, beavers, bears and trappers, and these men aren't any of those. It's hard to think of a good reason to find eight men riding behind us, maybe following us, maybe not, but I think it would be best if we didn't meet them.

I slip back down the hill, mount up and head to camp. Bill's already back, and the three of them are eating, looking comfortable enough that I know Bill didn't bring any bad news. I ride up and look at Bill.

"Take it you didn't see anything?"

Bill finishes chewing before answering, "Not a thing. Looks like we'll be the first ones through here in at least a few weeks. You?"

"Yeah, I did. Eight men, a few miles back. Not packing pelts, and not Indians. Felt like they're working our trail."

We're all used to trusting our instincts, and having ridden together for a couple of years, we've learned to trust each other's as well. They can tell I'm concerned, and this gets everyone's attention. All three of them look up at me, since I'm still sitting my horse.

Mississippi asks, "What do you think?"

I wait a bit before answering, "Could be anything. Could be a coincidence. But it doesn't feel like it. Kinda thinkin' these might be the pelt thieves we've been hearing about. Didn't expect to see so many ridin' together. I might be wrong about them, but I'd rather find out after we are safely at the fort. I think we need to put some miles behind us. I'll stay behind and keep an eye on them." I smile at my friends. "If you hear a gunshot, slap those horses and head to the fort. I don't want anything to happen to our pelts."

Mississippi, now standing, asks, "You want one of us to go back with you?"

"No. Not expecting gunfire, and whether it's eight on one or eight on two, we'd be in trouble. If things do go bad, you can each take a pack mule and maybe make it to the fort." I decide to skip eating. "I'll catch up with you just before the sun sets. Keep ridin' till then."

Just as I'm about to turn back, Oregon Bill speaks up.

"Dusty, you remember where the Y is? I showed it to you last year. Stayin' right's the easy way. Going left takes you to the Grizzly."

"Yeah, I remember." Bill had shown it to me and explained why we didn't take it, even though it's a little shorter way to get to the fort.

Bill continues, "Well, I'm thinkin' we should go left."

I think about what he told me last year. "Thought you said the Grizzly can run strong and isn't easy to cross."

Bill nods his agreement, then explains, "I did. But we haven't had much rain this year, and I think we'll be able to get across. Plus, I'm hoping these guys don't know that way and we'll lose them. If we can buy a few hours and shorten the distance to the fort, we may be able to ride in without a problem."

Mississippi speaks up. "Bill, it's your retirement, so we'll do it your way. Dusty, take the turn toward the Grizzly, and we'll see you tonight, or maybe in the mornin' if it starts to get late. That trail ain't easy to ride at night."

I nod my agreement and watch as all three men stand up and start to check their weapons, making sure they're clean and loaded and that they have plenty of ammunition close at hand. We're all hoping there's no problem, but hope's never stopped a bullet.

With a forced smile and quick wave, I turn to leave, shouting over my shoulder, "See you at the Grizzly, boys."

*****

I ride back to the same hill, which is getting awfully familiar. I'm even more careful working my way to the top this time, and when I peek over to the other side, I see they've gained more ground on us than I would have thought, or hoped. They haven't done anything except ride the same trail we did, but I still can't think of why they'd be here, unless they're looking for us. They slow down a couple of times, and it seems like they're looking for tracks, our tracks, but I might just be getting a little nervous.

I work my way back down the hill to my horse and start trailing Pete, Bill and Mississippi. Same thing these eight behind me seem to be doing. It must be about three hours before I come to the Y, and I can see in the fast-fading light that they did go left toward the Grizzly. Unless those eight men started riding faster, I'm about an hour ahead of them. I decide to ride down the trail a bit, tie off my horse and work my way back through the woods toward the eight men. They know that because of the pack mules, they're riding faster than us, so they probably figure they have plenty of time tomorrow for whatever they have planned.

Sure enough, as the last light fades into darkness, they come riding up the trail. I actually hear them before I can see them. I'm well-hidden, so I'm not worried about being seen. I can't make out their words, but it soon becomes clear they've decided to call it a day and set up camp. I'm tempted to sneak up close enough to listen, but decide not to press my luck.

I work my way quietly back to my horse. Sticking to the woods, I move alongside the trail until I find a small rise where I can set up camp, and in the morning, I'll be able to watch and see which way these men are going to go. With no food, and too worried about being seen to light a fire, I settle in against a tree and watch the light rain drip down through the huge trees.

I decide that if they keep going straight, I'll ride ahead, catch Mississippi, Pete and Bill, and let them know it turned out to be nothing. But, if they make the left and head toward the Grizzly, having no reason to do so unless they're following us, I will treat them as hostile. Trusting that they won't be sending a man, or men, into the woods at night, and trusting that my horse will let me know if anything, or anyone, approaches, I wrap myself in my bedroll and drift off to sleep.

*****

I wake up before the sun. I remember right away that I'm out of food, and I've now gone since breakfast yesterday without eating. My stomach is letting me know it doesn't agree with all of my recent decisions, but there's no way to hunt now and no time to trap. I think the others are out of food too, so they'll be grumpy when I catch up to them. It starts to rain a little harder, so I pull my coat tighter and start watching the trail.

More than the others, I spend money on weapons, and right about now, I'm glad I do. At the end of last season, I bought a new Harpers Ferry Model 1841 rifle. It set me back quite a few pelts, but the percussion model works so much better in the rain than an old flintlock. And being able to shoot a .54 caliber bullet two to three times per minute seems very valuable at a time like this.

Once I know the 1841 is ready, I take another look at my Colt Paterson revolver. A .36 caliber five-shooter should be valuable if they get close, but I sure hope I don't have to find out.

Having done what I can, including saddling up my horse in case I'm required to leave on short notice, I settle in to wait.

*****

They must have decided that today is the day, because I don't have to wait long before they come riding up. All eight are together, so they don't have scouts ahead or trailing. They ride up to the Y, and I watch closely, hoping they'll keep going straight and make my day easy.

I see the two in the lead lean left on their horses. It doesn't take much to spot the tracks of three horses and three mules, and both men look back at the other six and point in my direction. If I had any doubts last night about their intentions, they are erased this morning.

An idea comes to me. One last chance for them to reconsider. I take the 1841 and lay it out across the flat rock in front of me, aiming at the dirt a few feet in front of the two leaders. It's only about a half-mile away, so not a tough shot. It crosses my mind I could be all wrong about these men, and if so, when this is over, I'll search them out at the fort, buy them all a round and apologize. But if I'm right, every hour is going to count, and I'm hoping to buy some time.

I squeeze off a shot, a little closer to one of the men than I intended. His horse bucks and throws him, and he lies, unmoving, where he falls. The others leave him in the dirt and disappear into the woods. I alternate shots between the 1841 and my Colt, hoping they'll be confused and think there's more than one man shooting. They're firing back, but they don't know where I am, so unless they get lucky, I should be okay. My other hope is that my friends can hear the shots, remember what I said and start racing toward the Grizzly.

I stop shooting, but stay hidden and watching. After a couple of minutes, they stop too, but it's almost ten minutes before one of them works his way back to the trail where his riding partner still lies. I put a .54 caliber shot at his feet and send him scurrying back to the woods, once again abandoning the man lying still on the trail. This time, hoping I've bought enough time for my friends—and me—I race to my horse, ride through the woods for about a mile and then work my way to the trail, riding fast.

It's over an hour before I catch Pete, Bill and Mississippi, and it's obvious they heard the shots and have been riding hard. The mules are packed heavy, and while they're good, strong animals, they can only move so fast while carrying that much weight. We pull up to give the horses and mules a blow and for me to explain what happened.

When I'm done, Pete says, "Can't see any other reason, 'cept our pelts, for what you told us. The horses are okay, but the mules are getting tired. We're all hungry, since we ran out last night and didn't think we should hunt."

Mississippi jumps in. "Bill, I haven't gone this way before. How far to the Grizzly and then how far to the fort?"

He answers quickly, "Maybe three hours to the Grizzly, and at least another day, maybe even a day and a half, to the fort."

Mississippi looks around. "I guess we better start ridin'—fort ain't gettin' any closer with us sittin' here."

I look at Bill. "Should I stay back?"

He doesn't hesitate. "No. The surprise is gone, and even if you happen to pick off one or two of them, the others won't hide in the woods like they did last time—they'll be coming for you. Let's stick together and see if we can't make the fort, or get close enough these guys will quit."

The next two hours pass without conversation, incident or rest. A full day of riding fast, tension, and sleeping and eating little is starting to take its toll on all of us, and the mules are looking especially worn out. We haven't seen or heard the men behind us, but we know they're gaining on us and now expect to hear them approaching any minute.

Another half-hour passes and the horses are beginning to labor, subtly but no doubt tiring quickly. A glance over my shoulder shows the mules are staying with us, but will soon be fading. I don't think we can make it to evening at this pace, much less whatever we have to cover tomorrow. I'm just about to yell something about needing to stop when I hear, very slightly, the sound of horses behind me. I'm not the only one to hear it, as I watch Pete and Mississippi turn and look back too.

Fifteen more minutes pass, and the rain is coming down harder, the temperature is dropping, and the sound of the horses behind us is growing louder and louder.

Bill's in the lead and yells back, "The Grizzly's just a couple miles ahead." With that, he spurs his horse and brings it to a near gallop.

Right then, I hear the first shot fired, and if I needed any extra motivation, that did it. I drop my head down on my horse's neck, give her a quick kick in the side and push forward, the Grizzly coming into sight.

More shots ring out, and one of the mules lets out a terrible scream, stumbles and falls, never to get up. Moments later, we're at the bank of the Grizzly. Bill doesn't hesitate and plunges into the icy water, and we all follow.

As we get to the other side and back into the forest, bullets flying past us, Oregon Bill suddenly stops.

"That's it. I'm done. These are my last couple of days as a trapper, and if they're gonna be my last couple of days on earth, I ain't gonna spend 'em runnin'."

I look around and see that we've ridden ourselves and our horses to exhaustion. We're out of food and patience, and Bill's decided the time has come to quite running and take a stand. We obviously all agree, since we all dismount and grab our rifles, tying off the horses and the mules and running back to the Grizzly.

We quickly find positions behind rocks and trees and set up. There's only one place to safely cross the river, and we intend to make it very unsafe. They've been warned off and given every chance to give up, but haven't done so. It's clear they're not going to quit on their own and equally clear we can't outrun them all the way to Fort Vancouver.

I set my Colt on the rock in front of me and rest my 1841 against my shoulder, again thankful to not have a flintlock. It doesn't take long before they ride into view. The rain's coming down hard enough to obscure views, which plays to our advantage, and even in the couple minutes between when we crossed and now, the Grizzly has risen a bit, which will slow them down.

They stop on the bank, and I'm a little surprised to see there are only seven. Looks like the one who got bucked back at the Y was hurt more than I thought he was, and thinking back, I realize he never did walk or crawl off of the trail.

It doesn't seem to enter their minds that we might have stopped, so after looking at the river for a minute, they all start to work their way down the bank and into the rising water. The Grizzly's about seventy-five feet across at this point, plenty of room for all of them to be in the river at the same time, which is what we are hoping for.

It was agreed that since I have the only percussion rifle and the revolver, I would shoot first. I wait until the first three riders are about two-thirds of the way across and the other four are all the way in the water.

I close my eyes and take a deep breath, and when I open them, I take the first shot.

As soon as I do, Bill, Pete and Mississippi start firing. At this range, rifles and pistols are both effective. The seven men don't have a chance, but none of us felt they deserved one. None of the first three men even get a shot off, all killed in the first volley. The four behind them manage to get off a few rounds, but none of them leave the Grizzly alive.

It's over in less than two minutes. All seven men are dead, along with two of the horses.

As I look out at what we did, I see, for one terrible moment, Grizzly Creek running red. After making sure all seven are dead, I jump up to check on our men and happily find that none of us have been hit—even the horses and mules escaped injury.

The five surviving horses are still in the Grizzly, a couple of them panicking since the dead riders are caught in the stirrups. We all wade into the Grizzly and coax the frightened horses to our side. After checking for injuries and finding they have none, we tie them off with our horses, which calms them down immediately.

By now, the Grizzly has risen to the point where it would be dangerous to cross. The storm upriver must be huge. Bill looks across the river at the fallen mule.

"I'm okay about the pelts—we have plenty for all of us—but I sure hate losing that ol' mule. Had 'im for six years, and he never gave me a moment's problem."

We watch as the rising water picks up the last two dead men, who had both floated onto the opposite bank, and carries them downstream, food for the grizzlies and the coyotes.

Bill and I turn back and see that Pete and Mississippi already have a fire started.

Pete looks up and we walk into camp. "Good news. Took a look in their saddlebags, and those boys were well stocked. We're gonna eat well.

Figure everyone and everything is tired. Might as well set up here and ride in easy tomorrow. Even found a little coffee."

Mississippi, who enjoys a good meal as much, or more, than anyone, says, "Hated to have to kill 'em, but they left us no choice. Real glad they left us some food."

We all voice our agreement, and Bill walks over to his horse. He reaches into his saddlebag and pulls out a full bottle of whiskey, one we didn't know he had. I'm not even sure I knew he drank.

He walks back to camp, pulling the cork on his way as we all reach for our cups, which Bill generously fills. Skipping a cup for himself, he raises the bottle, and we follow by raising our cups.

"Boys, it's my last night as a trapper. It's been a hell of a life and a hell of day. I couldn't have asked for more than good health"—he takes a moment and looks at each of us—"good friends... and"—he looks back across the river into the darkness where his mule lies—"a good mule."

The End

Escape From Grizzly Creek

by

Cheryl Pierson

Scott Harris

"Grizzly Creek ain't too much farther ahead," Mark Thompson declared as he slowed his horse. His three companions caught up to him, all nodding at his statement, ready to at least be near fresh-running water.

The four had ridden themselves and their horses to exhaustion. They were out of food, water, and patience. With Mark's simple declaration that Grizzly Creek was nearby, it seemed they'd all decided the time had come to quit running and take a stand—no matter what the outcome.

Jill, Mark's younger sister by four years, was relieved at the unspoken agreement. It would be full dark in another few hours—barely enough time to get to the creek and find a good place to—*to try to survive.*

One didn't usually fight Comanches and live to tell about it... She pushed the thought from her mind. If they were to be captured, she could expect her brother to kill her before the

143

Comanches got them. She shivered—whether from fear or pure exhaustion, she wasn't sure.

Two days ago, their small settlement of Bender's Crossing had been attacked—and they'd been on the run ever since. The horses needed rest, and so did they. Their food supplies were next to nothing, but at least, where they were going, there'd be fresh water for all of them— horses and humans alike.

Mark, Jill, and their cousins, Andy and Ellis, had gone to pick berries for their families. They'd been spared during the attack. But when they'd returned to the carnage, they'd been spotted by a small band of the Comanche raiders.

And the Comanche had been relentless in their pursuit.

Now, they seemed to have fallen back a distance, and though Jill hoped that they'd given up, in her heart she knew better. *Comanches never gave up.*

At seventeen, Jill was the youngest of the group, and the only female. She'd managed to keep pace with the others, but it hadn't been easy for any of them. Ellis had probably had it harder than the rest of them, she thought, glancing at her bookish cousin.

With his fair complexion, the elements had not been kind to him. The July sun in Indian Territory was as unforgiving as the rough terrain they rode over. Even worse for Ellis was the fact that he was not a horseman of any natural skill. He spent most of his free time reading and daydreaming. He looked miserable and afraid.

His brother, Andy, rode beside Jill, stoically staring into the distance. There was not much opportunity to notice anything more than the immediate terrain and the tree limbs they tried to dodge. One misstep could be a death sentence for their horses and for them, as well.

Jill turned quickly to look behind them again as they rode. Though she prayed to God she didn't see those murderous painted faces looming near, she couldn't stop herself from glancing back over her shoulder.

Suddenly, they came out of the woods and found themselves on the banks of Grizzly Creek. The horses made their way quickly to the stream, and Jill dismounted, bending near it to cup her hands around the cool, rushing water.

The others drank deeply, then Andy stood and reached for his canteen.

"Good thinking," Ellis said, filling his as Andy and the others did.

"You know this area?" Andy questioned, glancing at Mark as he straightened up from the crouch and capped the canteen.

"It's been a long time," Mark admitted, "but Pa and I came down this way a few years back when we were on the way to Texas."

"You know of any shelter? A cave, or somewhere we could hole up till these damn Comanch get off our tail?"

"Pa said there was one back up that way." Mark nodded toward the west, the direction they'd come from. "But I'm not sure we want to go back that way to hunt for it. We may run into those savages we've been tryin' to outrun." He paused, then said, "We never could find it when we was here last. We got here after dark and couldn't see well. We just gave up and slept on the ground."

"We still got some daylight," Andy said doggedly. "Looks like it could rain—last thing I want to do is sleep out in the open with no cover. Hell, we didn't come prepared for any of this..." His voice trailed away, and he quickly busied himself checking his horse's feet, the tightness of the cinch, and making sure the saddle was as it should be. Busywork.

Ellis laid a hand on his older brother's arm, and Andy gave it a quick tap of acknowledgement.

They would all have to come to grips with their grief, with losing everything, when they had a chance to rest, Jill thought. By Mark's quick glance, the same idea was on his mind. He frowned and looked away. The wind picked up, and with it came the smell of smoke.

Jill looked at Ellis as he turned, a question in his eyes. She nodded. "I smell it, too."

"Do you think it's them?" Ellis asked, barely managing to keep his voice steady.

"The Comanch?" Andy asked. "Think they're buildin' 'em a celebration fire? Killed all our folks and now they're gettin' ready for us—"

"*Andy!*" Mark said sharply.

Andy whirled to face him. *"It's true, ain't it?"*

"Let's go see if we can't find that cave," Jill said hurriedly, hoping to diffuse the problem. Andy was hot-headed. He always had been, and he and Mark butted heads more often than not. It had been that way since they'd been children, Jill thought. Even before she and Ellis had been born. It was a family joke that Mark and Andy fought from the time they were born, only two weeks apart. Jill hoped they could avoid that disharmony, in light of everything else they were facing—and the fact that the four of them were all that was left on this earth of the entire Thompson family.

****

"There it is—I think I see it!" Ellis started up the side of the craggy hillside, dry dirt and pebbles sliding from beneath his feet as he awkwardly made his way to the nearly-hidden entrance of a large cave.

Jill gamely headed up the hill, too, following her cousin. She tried to avoid Andy and Mark, who were arguing again.

The smell of smoke had gotten stronger. Travelling back west, it was only a short distance before they'd spotted the cave. The entrance was large, but naturally shielded by scrub brush and taller vegetation. Once inside, Jill was relieved to see that it was large enough to shelter their horses, too, from the heat or a sudden rainstorm.

Jill's horse, Pepper, balked at being led into the entrance. "Come on," she coaxed. "It's cool in there. Time for a rest." She finally managed to get the paint inside, but the animal was still skittish.

"I don't understand," Jill said as Ellis turned to face her. He'd already managed to get his big bay inside and led him to the far wall. "Pepper isn't one to hesitate—"

"Jilly, I think I see why," Ellis muttered as he stepped around his horse, Mickey, toward her. Quickly, he knelt, and as Jill's eyes became accustomed to the dim light, she saw what Ellis did.

The outline of a man's body became visible, and she, too, crouched beside Ellis. Ellis managed to turn him over and her hand went immediately to the stranger's forehead.

He was burning with fever and losing blood. Belatedly, she realized one knee of the men's pants she wore was stained with it where she knelt, and her hand came away from the man's skin warm and sticky.

"Can you light a match, El?"

"Let's get some branches gathered so we can make a small fire. We'll be glad for it if it rains— it's so blasted dark in here, anyhow."

"I'll go—" Jill began, but Ellis interrupted.

"No. Let me. I can carry more. I'll get enough to get it going, and at least that'll give you some light to see what needs to be done. While you're looking him over, I'll go gather more to get us through the night." Ellis stood, hurrying toward the mouth of the cave.

"I wish I knew your name," Jill murmured in the darkness, shocked when the stranger responded.

"Matt… Duncan…"

*****

Jill jumped at the unexpected sound. "M-Matt?"

He groaned in response. "Who—"

"I'm J-Jill Thompson. What happened to you?"

"Kiowas… C-cavalry…"

"A battle? Near here?"

"Uh-huh… Grizzly Creek…"

Jill's thoughts raced. "How did you get here—to this cave? Did someone help you?"

At that, he gave a low chuckle. "Hardly."

Ellis brought in the first small armload of wood and knelt a few feet away in the center of the cave. As the tinder caught, the flames slowly began to burn. Heat was one thing they did not need on this July day, but light was something they couldn't do without, especially with a severely wounded man who needed their help.

"We need to move him, Ellis," Jill said. "Where are Mark and Andy?"

Ellis stood and brushed off his hands. "Where they always are. Arguing. Here, let me see if I can do it."

But Matt had passed out again, dead weight, and Ellis was afraid of hurting him by trying to awkwardly lift him from the ground alone.

Jill gave an exasperated sigh and headed for the cave entrance. Not wanting to risk calling, she started outside and was almost knocked down by Mark as he angrily stomped toward her.

"Mark, I need you—"

"Not now, Jill," he said, pushing past her.

"We've found a wounded man—"

"In here? In *our* cave?"

She stood perplexed, watching her brother, the ugly side of him coming out, as it so often did. "Where's Andy?"

"How the hell should I know? He got mad and took off on his own."

"*Where?*" Ellis stood, coming to join them.

Mark threw his hands in the air. "Said he didn't need us—he's going off on his own."

"He's trying to draw the Comanches away from us," Jill said. "We've got to go after him. There's a battle going on back there, according to him." Jill nodded in Matt's direction. "Andy won't stand a chance on his own."

There were a few seconds of silence, then, "I'll go," Ellis said. "He's my brother."

"No, I was the one he quarreled with, El. I need to go for him," Mark said. "This is my fault. I was stupid not to see through what he was trying to do." He started back toward the cave opening, but Jill stopped him, catching his arm.

"Mark, wait. Come help us move this man to the fire. Ellis can't do it alone."

"Huh?"

"The wounded man I told you about earlier!" Jill tried to keep the impatience from her tone. Mark was much like their father had been... he wouldn't tolerate what he called "sass" from anyone—including his own sister.

He heaved a sigh and followed her and Ellis back to where the stranger lay. "He's a bloody mess, Jilly." Mark grunted and groaned with the strain of lifting the muscular Matt Duncan as he and Ellis struggled to move him closer to the fire.

They carried him to a spot where Jill directed them and laid the stranger down. Mark turned to leave, but first, he took a two-shot Derringer from his saddlebag.

"Jilly, you take this, and if—if something happens—"

"I'll take care of it," Ellis said quickly. Mark wasn't speaking of any danger that might come from the unconscious stranger, but from whatever lay beyond the cave walls—the Comanches that followed, or whomever had started the fires they smelled as the smoke drifted on the breeze.

Jill took the gun from her brother anyway, as a kind of insurance.

Mark gave her arm an awkward pat, then shook Ellis's hand. "I'll be back, soon as I can."

Ellis nodded, watching him go. Tears rose up in Jill's eyes, but she forced herself to think of seeing to the wounded stranger rather than possibly just having seen her brother walk away for the last time.

She had begun to unbutton Matt's shirt when Ellis spoke. "Jilly, I'm sorry to leave you, but—I have to go after Andy."

Jill stared at him. *Why didn't I suspect he would do this very thing? But how could I blame him? Wouldn't I do the same for Mark? Especially now that everyone else had been taken from them. They were all they had left.*

Ellis stood looking at her, as if waiting for her permission.

"I—oh, Ellis—yes, of course." She gave a short laugh. "I'll be fine."

"I wish I could stay and help with—" he put a hand out toward Matt, "with him. But—well, there's no time, and—"

"Go." She flapped a hand at the cave entrance. "Just go, El. I need to take care of him."

"All right, then. You ain't mad, are you?"

No. Just scared down to my bones. And weary. She shook her head. "No. Go on."

She'd already moved to take the small medical pouch she always carried from her saddle bag. She barely spared Ellis a look as he led his horse from the cave into the deepening shadows.

Jill moved back to the fire and sat down beside Matt. She didn't like using the water in her canteen, but what else could she do? She was close to Grizzly Creek and could replenish it. If she hurried, maybe she could get down there before dark.

She'd have to work fast.

*****

Mark knew his cousin Andy would head back west. The smell of smoke was blowing in from that direction, and there was a greater chance of running into that Comanche band that had been chasing them.

Andy had picked a fight to give himself a chance to separate from them and lure the Indians to come after him. If he was caught, he'd surely suffer a terrible end.

As much as Mark and Andy disagreed, Mark thought of his cousin as a brother—they were family—close family. Now, he might be gone forever, like the rest of their kin.

Just before he reached a gentle rise, Mark dismounted and, crouching low, made his way to the top in hopes of being able to see the lay of the land below him. He was close enough to hear voice, cries of pain, whoops and shouts—and the blasts of gunfire.

As he gained the top of the ridge, he was greeted with a horrific panoramic view. Grizzly Creek ran red with blood from both cavalrymen and Indians. Still, the battle raged below, and as he glanced to his left, he picked out Andy in the tree line, meeting his grim expression with a mixture of relief and fear.

Andy made his way over to Mark, leading his horse, and the two stood watching the bloody scene below. Finally, Andy made a move to do what Mark had seen in his eyes—he was going to join the fight.

"Hold on," Mark said, grasping his cousin's arm. "What the hell are you doin'?"

"Helpin' those soldiers. I reckon right now, every gun counts."

By the hot fire in Andy's blue eyes and the determined set of his jaw, Mark knew it was fruitless to try and stop him. But he couldn't just walk away, either.

"Andy—this ain't our fight. We've got Ellis and Jilly to think of."

Andy's look softened for a moment. "You take care of 'em if I don't come back." He glanced back at the ongoing fray. "I have to go, Mark. You found me. That's all you can do. A man's gotta follow his conscience. You—can't understand why I have to do this, and I don't expect you to come along."

Mark put out his hand and Andy shook it firmly, then with one last look, he turned away. Andy walked his horse down the hillside, keeping to the tree line as best he could.

"No! *Andy—no!*"

Mark jerked around as Ellis rode up behind him. "Hush up, Ellis! You want to tell them damn redskins he's coming?"

Ellis looked at Mark with deadly purpose in his eyes. Before Mark could stop him, Ellis urged his bay forward into the openness of the clearing, following his brother toward the bloodbath below.

*****

As Jill finished cleaning the bullet wound in Matt's side, she sat back on her heels for a moment, thankful for a few seconds' rest. The bullet had passed through cleanly, a huge relief for her. The fire made the cave stuffy and hot, though it was still cooler than it would be in the July heat outside.

She'd had to leave for a few minutes, earlier, to go for more water for the canteen, but when she'd knelt at the creek...

She shuddered, remembering the pink tint to the water that, at first, she'd thought was only the reflection of the beautiful red, pink and purple sunset. As she'd looked more closely, she recognized it for what it truly was—*blood*.

Though Matt hadn't been in any condition to tell her more than he already had, there'd been a terrible battle of some kind, or he wouldn't be in the shape he was in. But how did he get to the shelter of the cave? Uneasiness crept over her at the next turn her thoughts took... did anyone else know he was there? Did others know of the cave's existence? If so, she and Matt might find themselves with company soon.

What if they came while she was gone? *Oh, dear God—she'd left him alone and vulnerable in the cave—*

Quickly, she rose and re-capped the canteen, glad she'd not dumped the remainder of the good water before she'd seen the blood-tainted creek. Her only thought now was getting back to him. She still had a little water left. Maybe enough to get them through the night if she used it sparingly.

And how could she do that when the man she tended was wounded and in need of all the water the canteen contained—and more?

That had been at least an hour ago, and she'd returned to find Matt Duncan lying where she'd left him. She'd finished cleaning the wound, then torn the bottom strip of cloth from around his shirt to use as bandaging. She applied healing salve she'd found in his saddlebags, then the strip of cloth to cover the wound and stop the trickle of blood.

As she worked over him, a small pouch around his neck caught her eye. She'd seen such before. A medicine pouch, filled with mementos, charms, and other items to ward off bad spirits or evil happenings.

Matt Duncan was... *an Indian?*

Anger rose up inside Jill so hot it rushed through her stomach into her neck and face. She'd saved an Indian! *An Indian, like those who had slaughtered her family.*

Tears filled her eyes at the memory of the sight she, Andy, Ellis, and Mark had been faced with as they'd rode into Bender's Crossing. The unholy quiet, save for the crackling flames. The lack of movement. And then, the bodies.

When Mark had started to ride into the yard, Andy had shouted for him to "Come on! Ride!"— and they'd all turned and ridden hell for leather back the way they'd come as a small band of Comanches had come pounding after them, their war cries on the wind.

And now, Jill had saved one of those red devils. It didn't matter that Matt Duncan had had nothing to do with the murders of her kin. It only mattered that he somehow shared their blood. And she'd used up the water on him, cared for him, and saved his life when those who were so precious to her had lost theirs.

Just then, Matt opened his eyes and looked up at her, and with a feeling of helpless dread, she realized that Indian or white, this man held strong power over her, somehow. Her future was more uncertain than it had ever been.

*****

"Thank you," he muttered, fighting to stay awake.

She nodded, and Matt could see her emotions roiling like churning waves inside her. When her gaze moved to the pouch that hung around his neck, he understood. "The fighting—is it... still... going on?"

"I—don't know. My cousin took off, and my brother went after him—" Her voice cracked, and she shook her head.

"Where's the... other one?"

"Ellis? He's my cousin, too. He followed them." Almost as an afterthought, she picked up the Derringer from where it lay, close by. "My brother Mark left this for me."

"You won't need it, Jill."

"It's for—for protection. Ellis was going to stay, but—"

"I'm not gonna... hurt you." He closed his eyes for a moment, then took a deep breath. The pain almost overpowered him, and he felt consciousness slipping. But then, a cool hand on his forehead pulled him back from the encroaching darkness. When he opened his eyes again, she was staring down at him intently, her blue eyes full of hurt different from his own. *What had happened to her?*

He'd no idea how much time had passed, but he knew he'd slept. Still, she looked worried.

"Trust me," he ground out.

"How can I? You're an—Indian."

Ah. So that was it, completely. Not that her entire family had run off and left her with a wounded stranger they knew nothing about—only that what she had discovered about him scared her more than anything else could have.

"My mother was Kiowa," he said slowly. "My father... white... Scottish."

Her sigh of relief was audible, as if being half-white made everything all right, somehow. Didn't she realize some *white* men could be worse than any Kiowa or Comanche? Men were men... "Did you get caught in the battle?" he asked.

"No. We smelled smoke. We had to find a place to hide. Comanches were after us—at least, we *think* they were Comanches."

"After you... Why?"

"I don't know, Mr. Duncan. I didn't ask them. They'd just finished murdering my family."

He fell silent. *No wonder she was wary... afraid.* "I'm a scout for the army. You have nothing to fear from me."

But she had questions of her own, it seemed. "How did *you* get here? From the battle, I mean?"

"Walked. My horse was killed."

"You were, too, nearly."

"Happens when both sides... feel you've betrayed them."

Jill shook her head. "I don't understand."

"Indians feel betrayed because I scout for whites. Whites... well, they just hate Indians because—"

"Because?" Jill asked as he cut his words off.

"Because we exist."

"My family was killed in cold blood."

Matt knew that was coming. "Jill, I'm... sorry. But—I didn't have anything to do with what happened. If I'd been there, I'd have done everything in my power to stop it. I don't hold with that."

He read the belief and understanding in her eyes.

"I guess it's not right to think of all Indians the same. But why would they kill folks like my family? Ma and Pa were good people. They never hurt anyone."

Matt reached to touch her arm, and she met his eyes in the firelight. "I've always been caught between both worlds. Both sides hate the other."

"Yet, you've got two parents, one from each side, that you love. That must be hard."

He smiled at that. "'Hard' is taking a bullet from one of your 'fellow' soldiers—accidentally, of course... and having a well-thrown Kiowa knife miss you by an inch... or less... all at the same time."

"Kiowa—but—*you're* Kiowa!"

"Think they know that? Or care?" He nodded toward the cave entrance. "It doesn't bother the white soldiers to shoot at me, either." He paused. "Thank you for—what you did. Saving my life. Even though—"

Jill shook her head. "Please, don't say it. I never realized... so many things, either. It makes me ashamed." She moved closer, then sat up straight, looking into the fire. "If Mark doesn't come back, I have no people to return to. I have no home left—" Memories of her frantic over-the-shoulder glimpse of the burning structures of Bender's Crossing rose up in her mind as she gazed at the fire, and she closed her eyes.

"Come with me. If you think you could bear to throw in with a half-Kiowa ex-army scout—at least, for a while."

She blushed furiously, his words calling up her earlier blind prejudice of all Indians. She was depending on this one to save her life, if it should come to that—as she had saved his.

"Please... I can't tolerate tagging along with you on a tether of pity, Matt."

He came up on his elbow, facing her. "You think I feel sorry for you? I'd be inhuman not to empathize with what you've gone through. And it's not over yet. We still aren't out of this safely. But... that's not why I asked you to come with me."

Jill was at a loss for words. And she had no clear-cut choices—not now. "I have to wait for Mark," she said stubbornly.

"Can't stay in this cave forever." His eyes held hers until she finally nodded.

"I don't even... know you. Not really," she said quickly. "Do you plan to leave the army, then?"

He gave her a grim smile, pointing a finger at the bandage at his side. "Time to move on," he said wryly. Before she could say anything, he went on. "My father owns a spread near Tahlequah, closer to the Arkansas border. I can take you there, where you'll be safe... and that'll give us some time to figure things out."

Again, the heat rushed to her face. Oh, Lord. She'd almost made a gol-durned fool of herself, assuming he was asking, in a roundabout way, for her to marry him. And why would he have done that? Her with her ideas about Indians that he kept proving wrong, and only just having met him so recently! What if she'd responded to what she'd thought—She shook her head. He was only offering to take her away from here.

She pulled her shredded dignity around her. It seemed that was all she had left, now. "If Mark and the others come back—"

"Jill!" Mark's voice sounded from the entrance.

*****

Jill twisted to see her brother glaring at her, an arrow protruding from his side. He panted heavily as he tried to keep his footing. His eyes went to the medicine pouch at Matt's neck.

"What the hell... you an' this damn *redskin* all cozied up—" He managed to draw his pistol but couldn't hold it steady. "A damn Indian!"

"No!" Jill stood quickly, starting toward him, but he shook his head.

"Ma and Pa are better off d-dead than to see… this," he said venomously. "I'm… g-glad Ellis and Andy don't know. Dead… they… in the battle…" he finished vaguely.

"Put that gun down!" Jill said firmly.

"I saved th-the last two bullets. For you an' me. Looks like you don't… need one. How could you… Jilly? *A half-breed.*" He spat the word from his mouth like poison, then sank to his knees.

"Mark—please—"

"First, *him*… then, *you*. I'm… done for…" He swung the pistol toward Matt, murder in his eyes.

But Jill pulled the Derringer out of her waistband and pointed it at her brother. "You drop that g-gun, Mark," she said. Her racing heart let her know it was only an act, a show of strength that was foreign to her. "I d-didn't save Matt's life for you to—to take it." She'd never believed she could stand up to her brother this way, but how could she let him do what he planned to do?

"Matt?" His mouth twisted from pain to hateful spite at Jill's familiarity. "You... whore..."

The hard set to Mark's jaw warned her he was going to pull the trigger. Wrong was wrong— wasn't it? She couldn't let her brother kill an innocent man. That was as bad as what the Comanche had done to their family. Was she good enough to shoot the gun out of Mark's hand? She only had time for one shot. There was no choice. She aimed for his body.

"Jill, no!" Matt shouted, just as she pulled the trigger.

Mark's shot went wild as he fell forward into the dirt, the blood loss from the arrow finally taking its toll.

Jill stood holding the smoking Derringer. She let go a gasp of pure horror and dropped the gun, running to her brother.

Matt somehow reached Mark at the same moment, and helped Jill turn him over. Sightless eyes stared up at the roof of the cave, thin lips still twisted in a mocking sneer.

"I'm sorry," Jill whispered. *"Oh, Mark, what have I done?"*

*****

"You didn't kill him," Matt said quickly, laying a hand on her shoulder in comfort. "This arrow did."

She shook her head, distraught. "I'm a good shot," she insisted. "I aimed, just like Pa taught me."

Matt pulled her close, turning her away from the body. "I know. But—he fell just as you pulled the trigger. Your shot never hit him."

"I couldn't let him kill you," she whispered. "That's not right. Not how we Thompsons were raised up, Matt." She pulled back, looking into his eyes, willing him to believe what she said. "He— wasn't right in the head... so ugly... so mean."

*****

Matt didn't argue. He'd seen his share of hatred in his life, and then some. Mark Thompson may not have been "raised up" like that, but there was no mistaking his intent, and the feelings that prompted it. *Ugly* and *mean* were perfect descriptions—and he didn't believe those traits were foreign to Mark Thompson. In time, Jill would see it, too, but for now, it was too raw.

And now what?

Jill was right—she'd nothing and no one left to return to. Matt couldn't leave her here in Indian Territory alone. And—there was that one action that spoke more than anything else might have. That telling moment when she'd pointed her gun at her own brother—and pulled the trigger. She'd been determined to save his life, but Matt was grateful Mark had collapsed before her bullet found its target. That kind of guilt could prove crushing to her, and to any kind of relationship the two of them might ever develop.

Jill Thompson had a strong sense of right and wrong—and that was a beginning, a good one. She'd tried to save his life twice—once when she'd bandaged his wound and cared for him beside the fire, and just now, when she'd taken on her brother.

Someone might've heard that shot. They needed to clear out before they were discovered. These woods would be crawling with any survivors of the battle... if there were any.

"Do you feel well enough to travel?"

Matt turned his attention back to Jill as she spoke to him. "I—we don't have any choice. We need to get out of here before someone discovers us."

"And Mark? Just... leave him?"

"No time to bury him," Matt said quietly. She moved to retrieve the blanket Mark and Ellis had laid him on earlier. "I'm sorry, Jill. We have to think of surviving, now."

Jill shook her head, a faint smile touching her lips. "We only *thought* surviving was what we did back in Bender's Crossing every day—you know, with just daily living. These past two days, surviving has been..." She stopped and looked at him, holding the blanket close as she tried to fold it. "It's taken up every minute." Her gaze went to Mark's body, her eyes widening as the tears gathered, and she looked away. "Please... let's go."

Matt stepped forward to take the blanket from her, but unexpectedly, she came into his arms, and the cover fell to the floor of the cave. Matt held her, her heart pounding close to his.

"I'm so afraid," she whispered. "I'm afraid of everything."

"Of me?"

She shook her head against him. "No. Of living... breathing... losing everything in the next instant. Being chased and waiting for an arrow in my back, or the horse to step in a hole and throw me, or running out of water—or not being able to save someone..."

Her head turned slightly, and he knew she was looking at her brother's body again.

"I only *thought* I didn't care if I lived or died. But, oh, Matt, I want to live!"

"Listen to me." He put his hands on either side of her face and raised her head, looking into her eyes. "We're getting out of here as soon as we can pack up. No more running from anyone or anything." He smiled at the hopeful light in her eyes. "There'll be regular meals, a dress or two—"

"It sounds wonderful," she said huskily, leaning to pick up the blanket. Quickly, she rolled up the cloth covering and tied it on the back of his horse. "You're not well. We'll go a little way, out from here, where it's safer... and rest."

He nodded, standing over Mark's body. "I'll go through his pockets."

Jill looked away, her face drawn. "Yes... please. If—you're able." She moved to begin to put out the small fire, leaving him only the dim light of the small camp lantern she'd found in his saddlebags earlier.

There wasn't much, but Matt was grateful for what he found—the money was little, but he figured Mark hadn't planned on spending those small coins when he'd gone out to help put food on the table that fateful morning. The tobacco might be useful for a trade somewhere along the way.

When Matt stood upright, his head spun, and he closed his eyes for a moment. Jill's hand came steady on his arm. He opened his eyes to look into her worried face and forced himself to smile.

"You may have to help me into the saddle." Instantly, he regretted his attempt to lighten the situation. Her expression became more grim. "Just a joke, Jill."

She turned away to take Pepper's reins. As they walked their mounts from the cave into the early light of the day, she turned one last time, with a gasp, as if to go back to Mark's body.

"There's no life in there, lass," Matt said softly, blocking her. "Life is out here—beyond the next rise, under the coming sun of the new day." He nodded toward the creek. "If we had daylight, you'd see that Grizzly Creek runs red with the blood of white soldiers and Kiowa warriors, alike."

He took her hand, and now could see into her eyes—eyes that, before, had held no hope, but now showed a spark of renewal and interest in what lay ahead. "Let's see what we can create away from this killing place."

This time, he saw she neither mistook his words for more than he intended, nor less than he'd begun to hope for, himself.

With so much loss all around them, a new start could only be hopeful—whether they forged the path ahead of them separately or... maybe together.

She smiled. "Need help?" She nodded at his mount's empty saddle, and Matt shook his head.

"No. I'll be all right."

She swung up onto Pepper's back. "*We'll* be all right, Matt."

He managed to get astride his horse with a bit more effort than he'd anticipated but gave Jill a confident nod.

"Ready?" He started off ahead of her, and she followed, both of them looking toward new beginnings far away from the banks of Grizzly Creek.

The End

Never Walk Away

By

Nerissa Stacey

The evening sun burned into my eyes, still as brutally hot as it had been all day, but now at just the right height to render me nearly blind. Just behind me, Kira was slumped down in her saddle, looking like she might fall off at any minute.

"Let's stop here for the night," I said. "We should be able to cross Grizzly Creek tomorrow, and from there it's only another couple days to your parents' place."

Kira straightened up in her saddle. "No. I want to keep going. I haven't seen my parents in over three years, and I can't wait any longer. Plus, I promised them we'd be there a week ago."

"I know you miss them. But we're exhausted. The horses are exhausted. And if we end up getting lost trying to ride in the dark, it'll end up taking even longer."

"Fine." With a flip of her long, golden hair, she climbed down from her horse. But the look she gave me let me know she was none too happy about it.

If I hadn't been there to stop her, I'm almost positive she would have kept on riding until the horse crumpled to the ground underneath her — and then she would have taken off walking. That was the thing about Kira. When she got attached to an idea, there was really no slowing her down. And while I'd always admired her seemingly endless willpower, there was no doubt in my mind that in a contest between her perseverance and her common sense, the former would win.

We made our camp in a small nook just off the trail, and Kira started a fire and some coffee while I tended to the horses. They were in worse shape than I'd expected, and I cringed at the thought of telling Kira we might need to give them an extra day of rest.

I didn't blame her for her hurry. It was hard for her to be away from her parents. When she'd moved to South Fork, the small town where I'd grown up and where she and I first met, she had never planned on living there for long without them. The whole family — Kira, her parents and her younger sister, Lily — had been looking for a new place to call home. But since Lily was barely a toddler at the time, the family didn't want to risk too much travel until they had settled on a destination. So Kira had set off with a wagon train to find the family their new town.

It didn't take Kira long to fall in love with South Fork, and she sent a letter home telling her parents the town was everything they'd hoped for and more. But the letter she got back changed everything. Lily had fallen ill, and her parents didn't want to chance making the trip until she was better. For the next two and a half years, Kira waited in South Fork while her sister's health went through seemingly endless ups and downs. Every time Kira thought about heading home, Lily would get better. But then, inevitably, as soon as Kira's family started preparing to make the trip, Lily would fall ill again. And then one day, in the cold of winter, Lily fell asleep and never woke up.

Kira had wanted to return to her family right away, but she also knew that making the trip in the middle of winter would be far too dangerous. When spring came, she had gotten a letter from her parents asking her to come home and help them prepare to make the trip to South Fork. And so, here we were, on our way to finally make her family's long-delayed plans a reality.

As I was standing there, trying to decide how to gently break the news to her that our trip might be postponed another day, the unmistakable sound of hooves on the dirt jolted me from my thoughts. Squinting into the darkness, I could just barely make out the silhouettes of two riders at the corner of our camp, not more than a few feet away from where Kira was sitting.

Cautiously, I began to walk toward them. Seeing me approaching, the larger of the two called out.

"Hello, friend! We want no trouble. We've been on the trail for quite some time, and we were hoping to stop and rest for a moment."

The other man added, "We ran out of food, and we'd be much obliged if you have any you could spare."

"Well, we—" I had been planning to offer them some hardtack and a bit of dried meat and then send them on their way, but Kira had other ideas.

"Please, won't you join us for the evening?" she asked. "We have plenty of food, and we'd love the company of fellow travelers."

That was the other thing about Kira. What she lacked in common sense, she made up for in compassion and trust. She had a way of seeing the best in people — and of bringing out the best in them. Truth be told, there were days when her radiant optimism was the only thing that kept me going. But right now, all I could do was hope her sunny outlook and unwavering faith in mankind weren't going to get us killed.

"Thank you," the second man said. "I'm Jacob, and this here's Steven."

"My name's Troy, and this is my..."

I realized I didn't know how to explain what Kira was to me. She'd been a part of my life for the past three years — ever since she'd first moved to South Fork. We saw each other almost every day, and I felt at ease with her in a way I never had with anyone else. But still, every time I looked into her big blue eyes, I got this feeling like my heart suddenly forgot how to beat properly. It was like she made me feel comfortable and nervous at the same time.

And yet I had no idea how she felt about me. I knew she saw me as a friend... but then there was that one time when I brought her a tray of fresh-baked donuts on her birthday. In her excitement, she'd wrapped me in a tight hug and kissed me right on the lips. We'd both just stood there for a moment, and then she turned bright red and started apologizing profusely. I'd wanted more than anything to grab her and kiss her again, but my nerves got the better of me.

As I struggled to find the words to introduce Kira to Steven and Jacob, she shot a questioning glance my way and came to my aid. "I'm Kira. It's a pleasure to meet you. Won't you please take a seat? I'll pour you some coffee."

The men settled in, and as the night wore on, we took turns sharing stories of our adventures on the trail.

"Have you ever had a run-in with One-Eyed Dave?" Steven asked.

"No, can't say as I have," I replied. "Course, I can't say I've heard of him either."

"Don't let him hear you say that." Steven and Jacob shared a look, and Steven continued. "One-

Eyed Dave is probably the most feared outlaw in these parts. For years he's prowled the trails that lead through the canyon, preying on innocent travelers. He'll take anything you've got — your money, your horses, even your life if it comes down to it.

"They say he was in a gang at first, but eventually the others got sick of him taking their share. They tried to kick him out, so he shot each and every one of them dead — all seven of 'em — and left their bodies in a cave for the animals to eat."

"I've never heard of anyone who ever got the upper hand on him," Jacob added. "Although I guess someone must've, or else he'd still have both eyes."

Steven nodded in agreement. "There was a group of four men a few years ago who tried to put a stop to it all, but in the end they met the same fate as everyone else. One-Eyed Dave had been following the men for days, taking a gun here, a sack of gold there — it was almost like it was a game to him, like he was playing with his food. After a while, the four had ridden themselves and their horses to exhaustion. They were out of food, water and patience and decided the time had come to quit running and take a stand.

"They made their stand at Grizzly Creek — not too far from here, actually. Anyway, they say the creek ran red with all the blood One-Eyed Dave spilled from those men. As for him? Rumor has it he walked away without a scratch."

Steven paused for effect, looking across the fire at each of us.

In response, Jacob stood up and, brushing his hands together as if he were brushing away the conversation itself, said, "No one's heard anything about One-Eyed Dave in more than a year, though. My guess is a bear or a wolf finally did what no man could. It's getting late. I'm turning in for the night."

The rest of us followed suit, but for me, sleep didn't come easily. I couldn't help but feel like a fool for bringing Kira out here. I knew there was always the potential to run into outlaws on any trail, but it pained me to think that a legend like One-Eyed Dave was on the loose, right in the area where we were traveling, and I hadn't even known he existed. I was the one who had picked our route. I should've asked around first. I should've planned to travel with a larger group. But I had been careless. And if anything happened to Kira...

I shook those thoughts from my mind, trying to focus my attention on what to do next. Crossing Grizzly Creek was the most direct way to get to Kira's parents' house, but going that way made us an easy target for trouble. If we stuck to the hills and avoided the canyon, we'd be harder to spot, and we'd be outside One-Eyed Dave's usual territory. But that would add at least an extra week to our trip, and the ride would be much more difficult.

For the rest of the night, I drifted in and out of sleep, plagued by thoughts of a one-eyed outlaw lurking in the shadows.

Jacob and Steven left at first light. Part of me had been hoping they'd be headed the same direction as we were — then at least we would have had the advantage of strength in numbers. But no such luck. They were headed in the direction Kira and I had come from.

By the time Kira woke up, I still hadn't decided what to do. To buy myself some time, I checked on the horses. As I'd suspected, they were in no condition to take on another full day of riding.

I headed back toward the center of camp and found Kira pulling on her boots. When she saw me, she stood up with a bounce. Hands on her hips, an excited grin on her face, she cocked her head to the side and asked, "You ready?"

She was darn near impossible to say no to. But, even more than I wanted to give her everything she wanted in the world, I wanted to keep her safe.

"Maybe we oughta slow down for a second," I said. "After what they said last night about One-Eyed Dave, I'm not so sure heading straight for Grizzly Creek is the best idea. If we took the long way around the canyon, we could—"

"Oh, come on, Troy. Those were just stories. Plus, even if they're true, Jacob also said it's been more than a year since anyone's had any trouble with One-Eyed Dave. Going around the canyon would add at least another week to our trip, and I'm not going to let some silly outlaw, who may or may not even exist, make this take any longer than it already has."

Maybe it was that I was tired from the long days on the trail, or maybe it was the slightly condescending way she said it, but I felt myself starting to get frustrated.

"Kira, do you think maybe you're being a bit naïve?"

"Naïve?" She looked like the word actually tasted bitter in her mouth. "No. I just don't want to live my life always worrying that something bad is going to happen."

"Well, then, I hate to break it to you, sweetheart, but you might not end up living long enough for it to make much difference anyway."

The usual happy light in her eyes turned to hurt and anger, and I could tell I'd gone too far.

"Fine. If you don't want to go, I'll just go by myself." Turning quickly on her heels, tears brimming in her eyes, she stomped off toward the horses.

In a last, half-hearted attempt to stop her, I said, "The horses are barely able to stand, let alone walk. If you force them, you'll barely make it out of camp."

She turned around and paused, and for a brief moment I thought I'd somehow made her see reason. But then, brushing past me with her chin in the air, she said, "Then I guess I'll just have to walk."

For a second, I just stared after her, marveling at her determination — and fuming at her stubbornness. Sitting down on a rock, I thought about what to do next.

There was never any doubt in my mind that I would go after her, but a large part of me really wanted to teach her a lesson first. Let her get a little scared. Let her feel the uncertainty of being alone in the wilderness. Maybe if she got a taste of the danger that was out there, she'd understand why I wanted her to be more cautious.

Suddenly, a scream shattered the silence, reverberating off the canyon walls and sending chills down my spine.

Kira. I was certain it was her.

And now our argument seemed so stupid. I silently cursed myself for wanting to show her the error of her ways. Feeling panicked and sick, I quickly felt for my Colt revolver, grabbed my canteen and took off after her.

For a short while, I could easily follow her tracks. But all of a sudden they disappeared. Considering the short length of time between when she'd left and when I heard the scream, the end of her tracks lined up just about right.

At that point, I had a choice — explore the woods on either side of the trail or continue following the path I'd been on toward Grizzly Creek. If someone had taken Kira — which seemed likely, given the abrupt stop to her tracks — hiding out in the woods would be the most logical next step for them. But I had no idea which side of the trail to start with, and a brief search on either side revealed no further clues. If I guessed wrong, I knew I could end up exploring in the wrong direction for days. So I continued down the trail, quickening my pace and hoping against hope that I'd come across some sign of Kira.

To my utter surprise, not more than a few minutes passed before I saw the clear, unmistakable tracks of a horse on the trail up ahead. They appeared every bit as suddenly as Kira's tracks had vanished. It made no sense at all.

I wanted to believe that following the tracks would lead me to Kira. But if someone took her — and I was almost positive that was the case — why would they have hidden their tracks at first, only to leave them completely visible a short distance later?

Then I remembered what Steven had said about One-Eyed Dave playing with his food. My heart sank to my stomach, and I pushed my legs to go even faster, feeling tired and sore and absolutely certain that with every passing minute my chances of finding Kira alive were rapidly dwindling.

As I walked, my thoughts turned to the first time I saw Kira, on what I found out later had only been her second day in town. I'd been eating breakfast at Lazy Joe's Restaurant. She'd walked confidently in the door, wearing a blue dress that matched her eyes perfectly and showed off her slim, flawlessly proportioned figure. I watched in awe as she walked toward the front of the restaurant — and was then pulled from my reverie as she promptly tripped over the leg of a chair and tumbled to the ground.

I immediately rushed to her side and helped her to her feet. In her embarrassment, her cheeks had turned a brilliant shade of red — and I remember thinking she was just about the most adorable thing I'd ever seen.

I invited her to join me for breakfast, and we ended up talking for hours. She told me about her family — how her mom had the heart of an angel, how her dad had taught her to fish, and how her sister, Lily, had a smile that could light up even the

darkest of days. And I told her about my family —
how both of my parents had died before I'd turned
twelve and how there still wasn't a day that went
by where I didn't miss them like crazy.

I'll never forget the moment when she stood up
to leave that day. She shook my hand, looked me
straight in the eyes, and said, "We should do this
again sometime." For the rest of the day, I'd
played those words over and over in my head,
hoping she'd really meant them.

The very next day, I ran into her again at the
general store, and we agreed to meet for dinner.
From that day on, we'd always been there for each
other — in good times and bad.

Now, as the sun began to set on the trail, my
hope of finding Kira began to fade along with it.
Although I refused to give up, it felt foolish to
allow myself to believe I'd ever see Kira smile that
irresistible, sly smile of hers again. I even found
myself longing to hear her stern yet gentle voice,

reprimanding me for what she liked to call my "unnecessary pessimism."

Then, a faint shape in the distance caught my attention. It looked like a large black horse, picketed just off to the right side of the trail. I continued walking toward it, my pulse racing with a mixture of hope and terror.

Sure enough, the tracks I'd been following led straight to the horse. And when I got there, a new set of tracks, made by a pair of large, heavy boots, took their place. Looking ahead, I could see that the tracks led to the mouth of a cave. More cautious now, I kept walking.

The closer I got to the cave, the more and more it began to feel like someone was watching me, like at any minute One-Eyed Dave would spring from behind the trees, testing whether I was man enough to stand and fight. But he never did. And before long I was just steps from the entrance.

My mouth dry and my palms clammy with sweat, I poked my head into the cave. The first thing I saw was the skeletons, seven of them, hanging from the ceiling. My guess was they'd once belonged to the men in One-Eyed Dave's gang. But now they just served as a final warning to other men who dared take a stand against the territory's greatest outlaw. Part of me desperately wanted to heed that warning and get out while I still had the chance.

But, as I continued scanning the cave, what I saw next removed any thought I might have had of escape. There, slumped against the back corner of the cave, ankles bound and hands tied behind her back — but still very clearly alive — was Kira.

She looked up, but as our eyes met, unmistakable horror darkened her face. She shook her head at me desperately, looking as though she wanted to say something but couldn't find the words. Before I could make sense of her reaction, I felt my arms jerked violently behind my back, held by a pair of rough, enormous hands.

A low, gravelly voice, accompanied by the smell of rotten, decaying meat, spoke in my ear. "That yer girl?"

Wrenching my arms from his grasp, I spun around, reaching for my Colt in the process.

The stories Steven and Jacob told had in no way prepared me for the man standing in front of me. At six feet tall and 190 pounds, I'd never considered myself a small man, but One-Eyed Dave towered at least half a foot above me, and his arms were roughly as thick as my legs. A mess of ratty, greasy, black hair hung around his mean, leathery face, and an empty, rotted socket sat where his left eye should have been.

Mustering all of my courage, I lifted my gun. One-Eyed Dave grunted a single, throaty laugh, and in one impossibly fast motion, whacked the gun from my hand.

"That yer girl?" he asked again.

"Yeah, what's it to you?"

"Makes it more fun that way, don't ya think? Here's how this is gonna work. Yer gonna give me all the money ya got. Then, maybe, I'll let you and the pretty lady go. Course, then again, maybe I'll just have a bit of fun with her first." He looked at me lazily. "So, whatcha got for me?"

"Nothing but this."

Lunging toward him, I shot my right fist straight into his gut. To my surprise, he made no attempt to hit me back. Instead, he calmly reached into his holster and pulled out a revolver. Smiling a crooked smile that revealed several missing teeth, he fired three shots straight into the ceiling as he took several large steps back.

By the time I figured out what was happening, it was too late for me to do anything to stop it. As the loose boulders and debris rained down from above, I hit the ground, trying with little success to protect my head. Finally, the dust settled, and One-Eyed Dave watched in amusement as I struggled to free myself from beneath the pile of rocks. With a great deal of effort, I managed to wiggle most of my upper body loose, but my left leg — which, from the feel of things, I suspected might be broken — was trapped between two heavy boulders that no amount of straining and shoving could budge.

I looked over at Kira. Her dress was torn, and she looked even more weak and tired than I felt. But I could also see her moving around ever so slightly, trying to discretely free her hands and feet without getting caught by One-Eyed Dave's sharp, unforgiving gaze.

Seeing me look Kira's way, One-Eyed Dave resumed his game. Crouching down beside me, he turned to Kira.

"Since it seems your friend has nothing worth taking, I don't see much point in keeping him around. Do you?"

With that, he pulled a sharp knife from his pocket. In the dim light of the cave, I could see the layers of dried blood caked where the blade met the handle. Slowly, I began inching my right hand toward my Colt, which lay on the ground ever-so-slightly out of reach.

My efforts weren't subtle enough. Seeing what I was attempting, One-Eyed Dave lifted the knife high in the air, violent glee glinting in his remaining eye.

"Wait!" Kira's voice bounced off the walls of the cave. "I was just wondering... how'd you lose your eye?"

For a moment, everything was silent. Asking that question was either the smartest thing or the stupidest thing Kira had ever done. I held my breath, waiting to find out which it would be.

One-Eyed Dave turned her way, lowering the knife. Slowly, he stood up and walked toward her.

"A dirty, good-for-nothin' woman took it from me. Her and me, we used to be partners. But she got greedy. Wanted more than her fair share of the cut. So I told her she could have her half, or she could have none at all.

"Next job we did, she tried to con me outta my share. So, I held a knife to her throat and told her if she wanted to live she better give me the gold and scram.

"But then she starts cryin' and carryin' on and apologizin' and sayin' she don't know what she'd do without me. For just one second, I let my guard down, and the next thing I knew, she'd stuck a knife in my eye and made off with the gold.

"That was the day I decided I'd never let no one take somethin' that was mine ever again."

One-Eyed Dave kneeled down beside Kira and brushed her hair away from her face with his gnarled, dirty fingers.

Whispering loudly in her ear, he continued, "But you know what? I never really did get my revenge. She was a pretty girl, just like you."

Leaning closer to Kira, he smiled grotesquely. "Maybe I'll take your eye. Maybe that'll help make up for what I lost."

He looked at me, then back at Kira. "Yeah, yeah, I think that's what I'll do."

Slowly, he raised his knife to Kira's face, running the blade lightly across her cheek. Somehow, I got the sense the game was over. He'd found his prize, and he was ready to move in for the kill.

Seeing no other option, I flung myself toward my Colt, hoping the momentum would free me from the rocks enough to reach it. Sharp, stabbing pain seared through my leg, and the world began to swim. Groping blindly on the ground, I felt my fingers close around the gun and find their way to the trigger.

One-Eyed Dave stood quickly and wheeled around, reaching for his revolver. With my last bit of strength, I lifted my arm and took a shot. The last thing I saw before everything faded to black was the bullet exploding into Dave's remaining eye.

I awoke with my head in Kira's lap, her gentle fingers stroking my hair. She had managed to clear the rest of rocks off my body, and from the look of things, she'd also fashioned a makeshift splint for my leg out of a few sticks and bit of fabric from her dress.

The fog in my head started to clear, and I sat up with a start.

"One-Eyed Dave? What happened?"

"It's okay," Kira said, pulling me softly back down to her lap. "Your shot made short work of him. I think it's safe to say he won't be bothering anyone ever again."

"How long was I out?"

"Just for the night. The sun only just rose. Rest for a while longer — your leg is in pretty bad shape."

We stayed like that for a while, Kira stroking my hair and me thinking how I'd be perfectly happy if I could just leave my head in her lap forever. But, once I had regained enough of my strength, I suggested we take the black horse and ride back to our camp to collect our own horses and the rest of our belongings.

I expected Kira to resist, to want to keep going at all costs. But to my surprise, she quickly agreed. My leg was strong enough that I could walk — albeit painfully — on my own, but she brought the horse to the mouth of the cave and helped me climb on.

The ride back to camp was uneventful. When we arrived, I was pleased to find everything just as we'd left it, except the horses looked much more rested than before.

There were still a few hours of daylight left, and although we wouldn't get far before nightfall, I figured Kira had waited more than long enough.

"Shall we head out?" I asked.

Her eyes lit up, but then she slowly shook her head.

"No, let's rest for the night and get a fresh start tomorrow. I think we'd be safer that way."

She was quiet for a moment.

"Troy?"

I raised my eyes to hers, struck again by their pure, perfect blueness.

"I'm so, so sorry I walked away on my own like that. That was a stupid thing to do. I knew you were right, but I was just too stubborn to admit it." Tears rose in her eyes. "I could have gotten us killed."

Sweeping her up in a tight hug, I said, "It might not have been the smartest thing you've done, but it did confirm one thing. You are, without a doubt, the bravest girl I know. Plus, in a way, I'm glad you walked away."

She pulled back from my hug and stared up at me, looking half hurt and half confused. "Why?"

"Because in that moment, as you were walking away, I realized I couldn't stand the thought of ever seeing you walk away again. I need you in my life, and from this day on, I promise to do everything I can to make you want to stay."

I picked up her hands in mine. "Kira, will you marry me?"

Wrapping her arms around my neck, she kissed me deeply, lovingly.

"Yes! Yes! A million times, yes!"

The next day, we headed out with the early morning sun, Kira chatting excitedly about how she couldn't wait to tell her ma and pa our good news, and me thinking how I had to be just about the luckiest man alive.

The End

The Miller Ranch

By

Tracy T. Thurman

Six men sat their horses on a tree-covered hill, watching the house below. Buck Reynolds, his brother Jason, and four others were on the run. They needed a place to hole up and rest a few days. They'd scouted out the roads and trails. The house was far enough away from the closest town to ensure no one would interfere.

It looked like an easy enough target. Surely there would be some money stashed away somewhere. They'd likely have plenty of supplies and probably some guns. There was also a corral with ten good horses.

They watched and took inventory. There were four kids—three boys and a girl. They'd kill the boys along with the old man. The girl and the woman would be bonuses. The men had flour sack masks tucked in their saddlebags. They decided to leave them put away for this job. There would be no need for them.

Ryan Miller was sixteen. He and his twelve-year-old brother, Joseph, forked out the stalls in the barn while their father tended the hooves of the horses, trimming and fitting new shoes. Tommy was fourteen, the middle brother—he assisted his father. It was a chore they enjoyed and one their father used to teach the boys farrier work—an important skill for folks who raised and sold horses.

Their sister, Martha, was fifteen. She spent most of her time helping their mother in the house. Cooking, cleaning and sewing, all the things a girl needed to do and learn. Their ranch was an orderly one. It provided a decent living for the family. Like any other ranch, however, it had taken years of work and sacrifice to get to the place they were. James and Nelly looked over their place and their children with pride and love. Prayers spoken in their house were always filled with thanksgiving.

The house sat in a lush green valley. The foothills rose to the south and grew into mountains as they meandered about and climbed upward the way that foothills do.

Ryan and his brothers, along with their sister, knew those hills like the backs of their hands. They spent their lives hunting, fishing, and playing among them. Ryan's favorite place was Grizzly Creek—a steep, rocky place backed by sheer granite walls. The creek was wide and flowed year round. Fast-moving cold water tumbled along over smooth stones and gravel. They never ventured away from the house without a rifle. Even young Martha was a dead shot with her .22 rifle. Ryan and Tommy had made themselves a sling just like the one David used to slay Goliath. They learned it was a very formidable weapon and had taken many squirrels and rabbits with them. It was difficult to master, but they had. They used the ancient weapons any time they could. They were quiet and saved ammunition, which cost money. Smooth stones were free for the taking.

The sun eased down into the lower quarter of the sky. Shadows grew out from the east side of the buildings and trees. Martha stepped out on the porch, wiping her hands on her apron. "Momma says it time for supper!" she hollered.

From the hill, Jason raised his telescope to his eye and leered at the girl. "My, my, my..." he said softly. The others chuckled wickedly.

James laid down his tools and went to pull off his leather chaps. He straightened his back and peered out at the hills. A reflection caught his eye. He'd looked at those hills for many years and had never seen any sort of reflection. His cavalry experience told him right away what it was.

The boys were putting away their tools and arguing over something insignificant. "Ryan, come over here," James said, watching the area that had caught his attention.

"Yes, Papa?" Ryan asked as he walked over.

James spoke quietly. "I think there's someone up there watching the place. I don't want to cause no alarm just yet. When you go to the house, get your rifle and your brothers and sister, go out the back, and come over here to the barn. Saddle your horses quick-like, in case you have to run."

Ryan peered around his father's shoulders. "You think there's gonna be trouble?"

"I don't know, son. But if there is, we need to be ready. For now, just do what you normally would. I'll tell your mother and the others once we get inside."

"We ain't gonna leave you," Ryan whispered.

"You'll do as your told, Ryan. If things go bad, y'all high-tail out of here," James answered sternly.

"But Father..."

James took Ryan's arm in a firm grip. "Don't argue with me, boy. Do as I say."

Ryan clenched his jaw and lowered his head. "Yes, sir..." The tone of his father's voice caused the hair on the back of his neck to stand up.

They walked to the house. James hurried them along. Once inside, he explained his suspicions. Nelly raised her hand to her face, covering her mouth. Tommy went to look out the window, but James grabbed him by the arm. "Stay away from there!" he ordered. He looked them over, then placed a firm hand on Ryan's shoulder. "Now do as I said. And keep quiet."

Ryan grabbed his rifle. The others did the same, taking their own weapons. Nelly shoved a sack full of food and handed it to Martha. "Just in case..." she said.

They made their way quietly out the back door and scurried to the barn. "Saddle your horses," Ryan told them. He was scared, but he didn't want his younger siblings to see it. He hid his face in his shoulder as he worked.

"But why?" Martha asked.

"Because Papa said. Don't argue. Just do it!"

They had their horses saddled within minutes. Practiced hands made the task go quickly.

Nelly looked worriedly at her husband. "Maybe they're peaceful," she said.

James shifted his eyes to the window. "Maybe. Peaceful folks don't generally watch a place from a distance."

The light was fading. Ryan peered around the door post of the barn. He saw the riders coming. They sauntered along, walking their mounts as if they were in no hurry. Ryan levered a round into the chamber of his rifle and stood back in the shadows.

"Hello, the house..." Buck called out. No answer came forth. "Hello, the house..." he called again. The men with him were all grim-faced and dirty. They looked around, surveying the property. Jason leaned over and peered into the window. They dismounted just as James stepped out of the door. He held a pistol tucked into the back of his belt.

"What can I do for you?" James answered.

Buck grinned. "We come a far piece, mister. Wanted to know if we might trouble y'all for some food and water. Maybe rest our horses and board up a day or two?"

James looked the men over. They were hard men. He could clearly see what sort they were. He forced a friendly smile. "We got no problem feeding hungry travelers, mister. Why don't y'all gather up right over there. I'll bring you some food. You can spend the night in the barn if you'd like."

Buck grinned and tipped his hat. "That's mighty neighborly. But see, we were thinkin' of stayin' in the house..." His smile faded then.

James shook his head but tried to maintain his friendly expression. He needed to stall those men as long as he could. Every second counted. Nelly held a shotgun just inside the door. She was trembling.

"I'm afraid there's no room in the house," James said.

Buck lowered his head and let out an absurd laugh. "There's gonna be..." With that, he drew his gun. James plucked his own weapon from his belt, but he was too slow. Buck shot him high in the chest. James squeezed off a single shot that went into the air before he crumpled to the porch.

Nelly screamed in terror. She dropped her gun in a panic and ran to her dying husband. "James! James!" she cried out.

Martha covered her mouth, screaming into her hands. The sudden violence caught them by surprise. When Buck fired his pistol, Ryan fell back against a post as if he'd been shot himself.

Buck grabbed Nelly by the arm and tossed her aside. She fell into the waiting arms of the others. She screamed out in rage as they pawed at her. James raised his head, weakly reaching out his hand to his wife. Jason shot him between the shoulder blades. James' hand dropped with a lifeless thud.

Ryan raised his rifle, sighted quickly through burning tears and fired. The .30 caliber bullet took Jason just above his right ear. His head exploded, showering Buck with his brother's brain matter and skull fragments. Buck staggered back in momentary shock.

Nelly fought the men who held her. She clawed and kicked at them. She was able to grab a gun from one and raised it to fire. Buck spun around cursing viciously, wiping blood from his face and shot her through the heart. She screamed in agony and collapsed. The men who held her tossed her away. Nelly Miller fell lifeless in the dust of her front yard.

"The barn! Someone's in the barn!" Buck yelled.

Ryan and Tommy fired at the men as fast as they could lever their rifles. The outlaws fired back yelling and cursing. "We gotta go, Ry!" Martha yelled.

Ryan's eyes were filled with rage and tears. Tommy cried loudly and fired his rifle until the hammer clicked on an empty chamber. Staying to fight would only end in all of them being killed. Ryan didn't care for himself. But he didn't want his brothers to die, and he certainly didn't want his sister to fall into the hands of those men.

"Go!" he yelled. "Go! I'll catch up!"

Tommy jumped astride his horse. Joseph and Martha were already mounted. They kicked the animals into a run and sped away. Ryan fired again at the men who were taking cover in the yard. He ran out into the corral and swung the gate open wide. "HYAW!" he yelled, chasing out the animals. The horses galloped away, kicking up clods of dirt as they ran. He swung into his own saddle and jabbed in his heels. His horse leapt forward, charging after the others. Ryan leaned down low as he sped away, bitter tears streaking across his face.

"Get after 'em!" Buck yelled. "One of them little bastards killed Jason!"

The outlaws mounted up, but their horses were already spent from the long trail they had been on. They made it only a few hundred yards before it was clear their own mounts were in no shape for a chase.

"They ain't gonna get far in the dark," one of the men said. "We'll trail 'em in the mornin'. Shouldn't be too hard to run down a few kids."

Buck reloaded his pistol and shoved it back into his holster. He knelt next to the body of his brother and frowned. "He was my only family," he said mournfully.

One of the other men rested a hand on his shoulder. "He was a good man, Buck. We'll miss him."

Buck stood and glared at the bodies of James and Nelly Miller. "Rotten clod hoppers!" he growled. He turned and looked at the house. "We'll bed down in here tonight then clean it out and burn it to the ground in the mornin'."

Five wicked and filthy men sat at the table where the Miller family once said grace before their meals. Nelly and Martha had the evening's supper already laid out. Buck and his men ate well that night. "Damn. That ol' gal sure could cook," one of the men exclaimed, leaning back in a chair.

Buck sneered at the men. He was angry and feeling mean. "Those little bastards killed Jason," he growled. "I'll bring 'em back here, hang 'em from the rafters in that barn and gut every one of 'em."

The Miller kids ran their horses to a place they knew at the high end of the valley. The ground narrowed and rose into a draw. It was sheltered from three sides with high rocks and thick trees. Ryan rode in right behind them. They tied their horses and collapsed into sobbing heaps. They clung to each other and cried.

Martha looked up at Ryan, her face contorted in anguish. "Why, Ry? Why would they do that? Why would they kill them like that?"

Ryan knelt by her and held his sister in his arms. She buried her face in his shoulder and cried. "I don't know, sissy. I don't know..." was the only reply he could muster.

Joseph and Tommy sat on the ground, their shoulders heaving as they wept. Joseph looked up, his tear-streaked face pleading for answers. "What are we gonna do now? What are we gonna do without them?"

"Do you think they'll come after us, Ry?" Tommy asked.

Ryan Miller looked over at his siblings. Being the oldest, they looked to him for guidance. "Yes. Yes, I think they will. I killed that one. They know we seen them. They'll come after us, all right."

Martha began crying again. "Oh, God, Ry..." She buried her face in her hands.

"Look here. We're gonna rest tonight. They won't come after us until mornin'. At first light, we need to get going to town. We need to get the sheriff."

"That's a long way, Ry," Joseph said. "We'll have to go back by the house to go that way."

Ryan sat and thought. "We'll have to figure a way," he said.

Tommy's tears dried up. He was glaring at the ground. "I don't wanna get the law. I wanna kill 'em myself."

Ryan felt the same way. "Me too. But those men are killers already. I don't know if we'd stand a chance against them."

"I don't care," Tommy replied.

Ryan took a deep breath and exhaled heavily. "Papa would want us to get to town. That's what we're gonna do. If those men get close, we'll fight."

Martha sat up and pulled Ryan's sleeve. "Don't let them get me, Ry. Kill me yourself if you have to. But don't let them get me."

Her words struck Ryan like a bullet in the heart. "They won't get you, sissy. I promise."

They slept fitfully on and off through the night. They didn't build a fire but huddled together as best they could to ward off the night chill. At first light, they were riding through the hills, looking for a way to reach the road without having to go past the house. The mountains were insurmountable. The hills twisted and turned in small ravines and arroyos. They knew the area well. There was a trail they could follow that would lead to the road. It passed close to the house but would be out of sight of it.

*****

Buck kicked the men lying in the floor. He'd spent the night in James and Nelly's bed. He was well rested. "Get up! Let's get after them kids. Take what ya can from this place."

They ransacked the house, emptying the cupboards with great, destructive sweeps of their hands. They found what money was stashed away, loaded up what they wanted for food and such, and broke things for the sake of breaking them. Buck took the guns and ammunition and passed them out among the others.

He stepped outside. The bodies lay where they dropped. "Find a shovel and let's get Jason in a decent grave," he ordered.

"What about those two?" one of the other men asked, indicating James and Nelly.

"Drag 'em in the house. They can burn with it," he sneered.

*****

They'd been on the trail for a couple hours. Joseph turned and looked around. A dark column of smoke rose in the distance. "Look!" he said, pointing.

The others saw it as well. "They're burning our house!" Martha said. They stopped and watched for a moment. Tommy gritted his teeth. Ryan clenched his jaw tightly. Joseph looked down, reaching across to take his sister's hand. He couldn't speak. The smoke twirled its way upward. Martha's lip trembled. "They're burning our house..." she repeated mournfully.

"Let's go," Ryan said finally.

They plodded along the trail. There would be a wide turn ahead. The road to town lay just beyond that. Once on the road, they would have to ride fast. Ryan surveyed their horses to make sure they would be up to what lay ahead.

Ryan tapped his horse into a trot. "Let's get goin'," he said. "We get to the road, we'll have move fast. Those men might see us there. They'll come after us for sure if they do."

The others followed suit. They were rounding the curve when a shot sounded. A bullet splattered against the rocks. Tommy glanced over and saw a man riding toward them. His teeth were bared, gun held out in front. A puff of smoke erupted from the barrel, the sharp crack of a bullet sounded next to Tommy's ear.

"I got 'em, Buck!" the man yelled.

Ryan shucked his rifle and snapped off a quick shot in return. He doubted he could hit the man, but he wanted to slow him down. The man ducked and swerved off the trail. "Turn around! Run!" Ryan yelled.

The kids yanked their reins and charged back down the trail. More shots sounded behind them. Bullets snapped the air around them. "Stay low!" Ryan called. They hunkered down, slapping their horse's flanks. Tommy suddenly wheeled about. "What are you doing?" Ryan yelled at him.

His younger brother swung from the saddle, dragging his own rifle with him. "I'm gonna stop that man," he said. His teeth were gritted angrily. The others reined up as well. A grave resolve settled among them. They were cut off from town. If they were to survive, they'd have to fight. Not later. But right now.

Ryan grabbed his rifle and took a place on the opposite side of the trail. "You two get back," he ordered Joseph and Martha. They faded back around the bend, but not far.

The man chasing them came around the curve riding fast, his bearded face alight with eagerness. Ryan and Tommy fired. Their bullets slammed into the big outlaw. His eyes went wide in shock, arms flailing as he tumbled over backward. He hit the ground in a dirty heap and remained motionless. His horse ran on.

Ryan approached the man carefully. He poked him hard with the barrel of his rifle. The man was unmoving. His eyes were wide, but he could see nothing. He was dead before he hit the ground.

"Got him!" Tommy exclaimed. He kicked the man's body.

"Let's get the heck out of here," Ryan said. They left the dead man where he fell and hurried away. "Let's get up to Grizzly Creek," Ryan said.

"We're liable to get trapped there, Ry," Tommy argued.

"No, we won't, but we can darn sure trap them," he said.

Their horses were all but played out by the time they got back to the high end of the valley. They had very little food and were almost out of water. Grizzly Creek was nearly a full day away. But they could make it as long as they could stay ahead of the killers who chased them.

*****

When Buck caught up to the others, he found them standing around a dead man in the middle of the trail. He shoved through. "What the hell happened?" he asked angrily.

"I don't know, boss. Larry here was up ahead. I heard some shots. Figured he'd got a couple of them kids. When I rode up, Larry was layin' here dead, and them kids were gone."

Buck shook his head. "I'll be damned," he spat. "Y'all let 'em get away?"

"They were gone. They ambushed Larry. I figured they'd have another ambush up ahead."

Buck swatted the man across the face with his hat. "They're just a bunch of damn kids, Ben! A bunch of damn kids is all! And you let 'em get away?"

Ben ducked his head. "They might be kids, Buck, but they done killed two of us," he explained. "Maybe we'd better think on this. Hell, we could be long gone before they ever got to the law or anyone else."

Buck eyed Ben venomously. "You wanna run away and leave these little bastards behind? They killed my brother and now they done killed Larry. I ain't gonna let that stand. You're gonna let a few snot-nosed kids buffalo you and run you off? Are you turnin' yella, Ben?"

Ben glared at his boss. "Hell, no I ain't turnin' yella, Buck. I just don't know if we oughta waste time on these pups."

"We'll waste whatever time it takes," Buck sneered. "Now let's get after 'em and keep your eyes open!"

They rode off after four Miller kids, leaving Larry in the dust of the trail.

Evening was settling in. Ryan positioned his brothers and sister about twenty yards apart where they could keep watch. "Watch the trails," he said. "If you see 'em let the others know, but don't make any noises. Don't shoot unless you just absolutely have to. They might just ride on by as long as they don't see us."

They hunkered down, hiding in the trees and behind large rocks. Fatigue soaked into them, making it difficult to stay awake. But each knew the safety of the others depended on them. Martha passed out a few biscuits Nelly had stuffed quickly into the sack. She could hardly bring herself to eat. The boys held the biscuits and stared at them, each with their own memories and thoughts of the hands that made them.

It wasn't long before they saw the four remaining riders approach. They were spread out, looking around, rifle butts resting on their knees, ready to fire on them on sight. Ryan made a low "pssst" sound to Martha who was at his right. She passed the notice along to Joseph, who in turn passed it on to Tommy. They watched them ride by. Ryan felt hatred swell up inside his chest. He could level his rifle and take one of them out before the others would know what happened. He resisted the urge, however. If the bandits charged them, there was no way he could ensure the safety of his siblings. They were afraid, but they were also angry. Martha trembled at the sight of the men.

Night closed in. Buck and the others had ridden back to the Miller place. The house was a smoldering heap. "We'll lay up here in this barn,"

Buck said. "Let them kids stay out there in the cold. Maybe it'll shrink 'em up a little."

"We'll get 'em tomorrow," Ben said with a sneer.

Ryan stared up at the tree tops, watching the stars overhead. He was working out a plan to get those men in a position where they could be taken down. Grizzly Creek was the place to do it. If everything would go right.

At first light, Ryan briefed the others on what he had figured out. They would need to lead the killers up past the first tree line. They would have to abandon their horses at that point. Just beyond that, the trees thinned out, and the ground was rocky and steep. The terrain rose on both sides, making a funnel-like area. Grizzly Creek was just beyond with a high rock wall behind it. There were many places to hide if someone knew the area. They saddled up and prepared to make their way across the valley. They needed to get to the far side and climb up to where Ryan thought their best chances would be. "We gotta be careful and quiet," Ryan told them. "Don't use your guns until they get to the creek."

There wasn't much of a chance they could escape, and any help was far away, if it were to come at all.

Over the last few days, they'd ridden themselves and their horses to exhaustion. They were out of food, water, and patience. They decided the time had come to quit running and take a stand.

Crossing the open valley floor was a risk they had to take. They almost made it. A loud "Whoop!" sounded in the distance behind them, followed by gunshots. The bullets snapped the air close to them but went wide.

"There they are!" Ben shouted. He drew his pistol and fired. Buck and the others did as well. "We got 'em now! They'll get lost up in those hills.

All we gotta do is pluck 'em out one by one," Buck growled.

Ryan rode in front, Martha was right behind him. Joseph and Tommy followed. They stayed low in their saddles as they worked their horses through the trees. The sounds of the men pursuing them fell behind them.

When they reached the first tree line, they yanked their weapons from their saddles and slapped the horses away. Tommy knew right where to go and hurried to take his position. Joseph ran with Martha, carrying their rifles. The two crossed the creek and ducked behind a couple of large boulders.

Ryan took a position across from Tommy in a cluster of trees. They hunkered down and waited, catching their breath. Ryan scanned the ground and grabbed a handful of smooth stones.

Tommy peered around. He could see his brother. His heart pounded in his ears. Ryan looked over at him and nodded grimly. He stretched the sling of his rifle across his chest and made ready.

The men cussed and panted as they stomped up the steep rise. The ground was rocky, making it difficult for a man accustomed to being horseback. The trees thinned out. They could hear the sound of running water up ahead.

Buck looked at them and motioned for them to spread out. Each one held his gun in his hand.

Ryan and Tommy heard them approach at the same time. They would have to move quickly.

Ryan saw the first man come from the trees. He nestled a stone into the leather pouch of his sling, wrapped the end of the anchor chord tightly on a finger and began swinging the weapon above his head. He swung it faster and more forcibly with each revolution. The man paused and looked about. Ryan flung the stone hard and straight. He held another stone in his free hand ready to finish the job.

Ben emerged from the tree line, looking about. He was bent over slightly in a crouch. He heard a faint swishing sound like something being swung rapidly in the air. Ben stood and craned his neck, trying to follow the sound. The stone struck him with the force of a hammer just above his left eye. *Thunk*!

"GAAAA!" he cried out. His gun fell to the ground as he clutched the wound and sank to his knees. He leaned over in pain when the second stone impacted the top of his head. The last thing Ben heard on this earth was his own skull giving way with an audible *crunch*. He sprawled in the grass, blinking his eyes until the light faded dead away.

Ryan ran to the creek bank and waited.

The others heard Ben yell. Buck growled and glanced around. "Where are ya?" he called out. No sound came forth. The other man to the right walked out, looking to his left.

Tommy leapt up on a rock, twirling his sling with growing force over his head and let fly. He reloaded and repeated the action two more times before a gunshot splattered on the rock next him.

A smooth, round stone struck the outlaw just above his ear. *Whack!* "YEEOW!" he exclaimed, falling to the ground. Another rock struck him in the face, shattering his eye socket. Another hit him again in the top of his head as he leaned over on the ground. He crumpled in place, blood oozing from the wounds. The man's ears rang loudly inside his head, then faded until he heard no more.

Buck caught a glimpse of Tommy and snapped off a shot with his pistol. The bullet struck to Tommy's right. Tommy jumped back into the trees and ran to the creek bank opposite Ryan.

Buck trotted over to where Ben lay on the ground. His head was swollen and misshapen.

Buck grumbled and cussed. "Damn you rotten little bastards!" He turned to the other man; his partner leaned over him. "How bad is he hurt?" Buck called out.

"He ain't dead yet. But he's hurt bad. That kid whopped him good, Buck. Looks like his skull is busted."

Buck stomped forward. He splashed into the ice cold water of Grizzly Creek. His anger was burning into a blood-thirsty fury. "Come on out here!" he yelled. "Come on out here, so's I can tear you apart!"

The other man trotted to catch up with his boss. Martha and Joseph sighted their rifles on him. They pulled their triggers simultaneously, sighted and fired again, then jumped to the sides of the big rocks.

Two .22 caliber bullets punched through the man's chest. The small reports echoed *pop-pop*. The man clutched his chest, staggering back a couple steps. He pulled his hands away, staring in disbelief at the blood that coated them. "What the hell...?" *Pop-pop* came more reports. Those two crashed through his forehead. The man's eyes rolled back in his head. He swayed drunkenly then fell like an old plank onto his back.

Buck saw where the rifle shots came from. He leveled his gun and fired into the gap behind the boulders until the hammer fell on a spent cartridge. He growled, grabbing fresh rounds from his belt to reload.

Ryan stepped out from the trees on Buck's left. Tommy stepped out on Buck's right. Both youngsters had their rifles trained on him, their faces grim and determined.

Buck looked about. He tried to hurry loading his gun, but it was no use. The two brothers fired. Their bullets smashed through Buck's ribs, shredding his lungs. The big man faltered, bloody froth coughing from his mouth and nose. The brothers fired repeatedly, emptying their rifles into the man who killed their parents.

Buck Reynolds lay dead, face down in the icy water. Grizzly Creek ran red with the blood of a killer.

The End

The Grizzly Creek Massacre

By

Russ Towne

Scott Harris

We rode our horses and ourselves to exhaustion. The four of us was out of food, water, and patience. It was time to make a stand. No more runnin'.

While we waited for the attack that we doubted we'd survive, I thought back on all that had happened to lead me here.

I joined up in the cavalry when news came that my older brother, Horace, had died with Custer and about four hundred others at some place called the Little Big Horn. A year too young and big for my age, I didn't want to wait to enlist on account o' bein' afraid the redskins would be wiped out before I was old enough to help chase 'em down and whip 'em. I told the army I was two years older than I was. Figgered they might think I was lyin' if I only added one year, but they probably wouldn't figger a boy would try to stretch the truth *that* far.

Well, we did a whole lotta chasin'—up, down, and sideways—but it seemed to me them redskins did most of the whippin'. They had us chasin' our tails.

We always seemed to get there too late to help settlers, miners, wagon trains, and the like, but not too late to see the things the savages did to white men and women. To this day, I have a hard time gettin' those awful sights and smells outta my head.

And while we was buryin' the poor folks, the redskins were off torturin' and murderin' someone else, or turnin' around and attackin' us, and then runnin' away before we could return the favor.

I used to think they was cowards, but they was just fightin' the only way they had any chance of winnin'.

I met Clem shortly after I enlisted. Three soldiers was makin' fun of him 'cause he'd been in for seven years and was still a private. I guess he was used to such cruelty, 'cause he treated them like they was just annoyin' flies that wasn't even worth swattin' at.

Clem's a big man, but somethin' ain't right with him. I heard tell that a horse kicked him in the head when he was five.

Anyways, it never sits right with me to see bullyin'. I couldn't just leave it be, so I walked up to the three and told them to stop it. They stopped bullyin' him all right and lit in on me. Next thing I know, Clem roared like the big bear he is and rushed those poor fellas. Not one of 'em was left standin' when he was done. I helped, but, truth is, I probably was more in the way than helpful. He was fast and real strong. When Clem punched someone, they stayed down.

That little dust-up earned all five of us time in the guardhouse and on shit detail, cleanin' up after horses. Brother, the cavalry has a *lot* of horses. From then on, the other three stayed as far away from Clem and me as they could, which suited us fine.

Ever since then, Clem has stuck to me like a shadow. We watch each other's backs.

We was part of B Troop. Our lieutenant was Lance Dittmer. He was what the other troopers called a "shavetail," 'cause he was fresh outta college and new to the army.

The cavalry shaves the tails of horses given to fresh recruits. It helps remind everyone that the men ridin' them ain't yet used to military ways, and may even be new to ridin' horses, so give 'em extra room 'til they been trained proper-like.

Lt. Dittmer didn't seem like a bad sort, but even a new trooper like me could tell he was awful green.

Our sergeant, Butch Henry, had been in for nineteen years and knew just 'bout everythin' there was to know about bein' in the cavalry. Trouble was, whenever we was away from the fort, the sergeant seemed to go out of his way to cut down the lieutenant. At first, he only did it behind his back, but then he started doin' it in front of the lieutenant in foxy ways with double meanin's. But everyone knew which way he meant. The lieutenant tried to call him on it a coupla times, but each time the two of them walked outta earshot to discuss it in private, the lieutenant seemed even more scared of him when they returned. Soon the lieutenant didn't even try to stand up for himself.

Anyways, we was on our way to meet up with a wagon train to escort it through an area where the redskins were thicker 'n molasses and hotter 'n hornets when we heard gunshots. The lieutenant gave the command, and we raced toward the trouble. As usual, we got there too late, but this time just barely. A miner had two arrows in his stomach, and a redskin was bendin' over him with a knife. The savage saw us, screamed what I guess was a war cry, leaped on his horse, and skedaddled after the other savages.

The lieutenant ordered the sergeant to pick four men and stay with the miner while the rest went off chasin' the redskins. Sergeant Henry picked me and Clem and two others to stay with him. We dismounted, and the sergeant told Clem and the other two to make a perimeter and keep their eyes and ears peeled for redskins. He looked at me and ordered, "Private Fernley, check on the miner. See if he's alive."

I did as I was told. The miner was still breathin'. His scraggly gray beard had grease from his breakfast in it. He'd lost a lot of blood but was tryin' to say something. Sergeant Henry came and kneeled close enough so's he and I could hear what the miner was tryin' to tell us.

The words came out as broken, raspy whispers. "I know... my time's up. Dad-blamed luck. I hit... the motherlode. Hid a big pot, full... gold dust... nuggets... hollow tree... south bank... double bend... in Eagle River..."

He pointed in a shaking finger at a mountain in the horizon. "Near pile... three flat stones. No good... to me... now."

One final exhale and he was gone.

The sergeant said, "The old fool must have been delirious. Still..."

He stopped to check the miner's pockets and gear and found a leather bag stuffed full of something. He opened the drawstrings and poured some of the contents into the palm of his hand. It glittered in the sunlight. He looked to look at me. Our noses was almost touchin', and I could smell his breath. Flying drops of spittle made me lean back a mite as he warned, "I'll kill you if you breathe a word of this to anyone. You hear me, boy?"

I nodded, shooin' away flies that had begun to gather around the miner. I think he musta been waitin' to let his threat sink in. As I waited for orders, I used my sleeve to wipe sweat from my forehead. The uniforms they gave us was way too hot in the summer and not nearly warm enough in the winter.

"Now go stand watch with the others."

The sergeant walked up to us a few minutes later. He ordered Clem and me to bury the miner. Then he took the other two men out of earshot. I knew they was extra friendly with him 'causes he sometimes used 'em as enforcers when he wanted to pick on people. Which was often.

When the lieutenant and the rest of the troopers returned without havin' caught or even *seen* the attackers, the sergeant reported, "The miner said the redskins are holed up at the double bend on the south bank of Eagle River. He died, and we buried him."

The lieutenant said, "I'd love to go after those hostiles, but my orders are clear. We're to escort the wagon train through hostile territory."

I wondered why he took the time to chase the redskins who killed the miner if his orders was to escort the wagon train, but I guess he was so hot under the collar at what they did to the miner—and so close by—that he just couldn't help himself.

The lieutenant pulled out a map but couldn't seem to make heads or tails out of it. "Sergeant, do you know where Prairie Junction is?"

"Yessir."

"Which way?"

The sergeant pointed toward the mountain. I knew something was wrong. Before the sergeant heard about the gold at Eagle River, we'd been ridin' with the mountain to our right, but now we was gonna be ridin' straight toward it.

The lieutenant didn't notice, and anyone else who did didn't dare say anything. So, off we rode toward the mountain, the lieutenant in search of redskins and the sergeant in search of something of a different color entirely. And, if the miner wasn't lyin' or hallucinatin', a whole lot of it.

I had time to think as we rode. I'd heard somewheres that gold was heavy. Never havin' held any myself, I had to take their word for it. Seemed to me that a big pot full of gold would be too heavy for a man to carry, mebbe even too heavy for a coupla mules if the pot was big enough.

I figgered the miner musta hidden most of the gold and just taken the pouch with him, probably to get it assayed and to hire men he trusted to fetch the rest of it back to town with him.

I got a sick feelin' in my gut when I thought how hard the miner musta worked to get all that gold, and then got himself killed just as he was 'bout to get rich. Didn't seem right that someone like the sergeant would get rich off the miner's hard work.

The sergeant pulled more of his buddies aside every time we stopped to rest the horses or for a meal.

There was two other new recruits besides Clem and me. The sergeant didn't talk with any of us, and he ignored Lt. Dittmer. I took that as a bad sign and figgered maybe I should powwow with the other new recruits and Clem, in case the sergeant had bad designs for us. The sergeant always kept his favorite men between the lieutenant and me, so I couldn't warn him, but they let us new recruits do as we pleased once our work was done.

I met with Clem, Donnel, and Kelby while the sergeant was having his powwows with his buddies. I explained what the miner had said and the sergeant was doin'.

"I think somethin's gonna come to a head real soon between the sergeant and lieutenant. The sergeant's talked to everyone but the lieutenant and us. He don't want to split the gold with us and won't want us as witnesses to whatever's gonna happen 'tween Lt. Dittmer and him. Be ready to ride fast and hard when whatever's gonna happen happens. Hopefully, we can surprise 'em and get away without gettin' shot. We'll head toward Prairie Junction. I heard that's where we was goin' before the sergeant redirected us.

"They're gonna hafta come after us 'cause of what we know, but I figger they'll wanna divvy up all that gold first. That should give us time to put some distance between them and us. And mebbe the gold will be so heavy that it will slow 'em down. Are you with me, boys?"

Clem said, "I go where you go, Luke."

Kelby nodded gravely, and then joked, "So much for my army career. Like as not I'll get shot whether I stay or go with you boys. If the army doesn't shoot me, the sergeant or Indians will. At least the three of you won't shoot me in the back. Leastwise, not on purpose." He smiled when he said that to let us know he was just foolin', and then said, "I'll hang my hat with you boys."

Donnel said, "The farther I can get away from Sergeant Henry, the better. I haven't forgotten the beating his thugs gave me for failing an inspection the first week I joined the troop."

The following morning, the sergeant led us to a large double bend in on the south bank of the Eagle River. He ordered, "Halt! Spread out and look for the pile of rocks and the tree I told you about. Shout when you find it."

The lieutenant rode up to the sergeant. "Why are we stopping? I didn't order a halt. Why are the men dispersing?"

Dittmer's eyes grew wide when he saw the Colt revolver in the sergeant's hand.

"I'm done taking orders from you, you dumb, yellow-bellied shavetail."

He shot his commanding officer in the face with about as much emotion as if he'd stepped on

271

a ladybug, and then turned toward me. I was too close for him to miss.

"Over here!" one of the troopers shouted, probably saving my life. Sergeant Henry yanked the reins to turn his horse 'round as he and all the troopers, but us four new recruits, raced toward the gold.

I whispered, "Now, boys!" We skedaddled as fast as our horses could carry us and rode for quite a spell.

We stopped when we crested a big hill to see if anyone was chasin' us. I'd guessed right. No one was tailin' us yet. The only thing they cared about was gettin' their share of the gold. That would change as soon as they had it and remembered we was the only witnesses to murder and mutiny.

I asked the others, "Any of you familiar with these parts?" They all shook their heads.

"Me neither, but before the sergeant misled us, we was headin' catty-corner to that mountain toward a place called Prairie Junction. I figger there will be people there, including the wagon train we was supposed to escort, and probably no army units. If there was, they probably wouldn't have needed to order us to escort the wagon train.

"Like it or not, we're deserters now, boys. We're gonna need to get outta these uniforms, get regular clothes, and change our names. If we're lucky, the redskins will find and kill Butch Henry and the other men before the army goes lookin' for all of us.

If the army finds Butch Henry first, he'll say we killed Dittmer, mutinied, and deserted, and that he and the others was trackin' us down to bring us to justice. The army'll believe them over us, 'cause we'll be the ones who are missing. If they capture us, I have a feelin' that, first chance he and the rest get, they'll make sure we get killed tryin' to escape.

"Addin' to the fun, the redskins are still out there. They'd like nothin' better than to torture 'n' kill them some soldier boys."

Kelby said, "If we stick together, we'll have a better chance of fightin' off whoever finds us, but we won't be as easy to track if we split up. If we go our separate ways, some of us might get out of this alive, but the rest of us will be easier to pick off."

Clem said, "I'm stickin' with you, Luke."

Donnel said, "You've kept me alive so far when by now I'd probably already be dead, so I'll string along with you."

Kelby nodded and said, "In for a penny, in for a pound."

"Okay, we stick together and take our chances."

We kept close watch on our back-trail. The next time we crested a ridge, we saw a dust cloud trailin' us.

"Well, boys, it's now a race to see who catches and kills us first, Henry's gang or the Indians."

Donnel said, "If we're gonna get caught, I hope it's the sergeant. I'd like to have a shot at that bastard before I die."

We all felt that way.

Once, when we dismounted to give our horses a break, Kelby began calling us the Four Musketeers. He said he read about musketeers in a book when he was in school.

"Some Frenchie wrote it." We listened as Kelby started tellin' us what he remembered of the story. I'd love to read that book and thought, *Maybe, someday I'll learn to read if I live through this.* It struck me that our story might be kinda interesting, too, so long as I was readin' it and not livin' it.

Later, Donnel started calling us "The Four Mutineers."

I said, "But we didn't mutiny, we deserted."

"I know, but the 'Four Deserters' just don't have the same ring to it as the 'Four Mutineers.'"

I had to agree with him.

We rationed what little water and food we had: about half a canteen of water each, and dried beef and hard tack. We'd had no time to grab victuals from the supply wagon.

We shared our water with our horses. That used it up faster, but we'd last longer with horses and no water than we would t'other way 'round. We did find a little stagnant water the horses drank without gettin' sick, but it was unsafe for us. The horses also grazed on good green grass.

Dried beef and hard tack aren't much fun to eat, but no fun at all to chew without water. But we was soon reminded that worse than that was no food and no water.

We cold camped. Didn't want anyone spotting our fires. Two of us stood watch while the other two slept. We changed watch every four hours.

The nights were cold, and the days hot and long.

We crested a small, U-shaped hill. Below us on the open part of the U was a creek. We looked back and saw a dust cloud probably made by Henry's gang. They were still quite a ways away but based on how much dust they was kickin' up, must have been ridin' hard.

If we stayed near the top of the hill, we'd be on the high ground and better able to defend ourselves, but without water. There wouldn't be time to get the water and climb back up the hill before they reached the high ground. They could surround us, get water from the creek, and wait 'til we died of thirst. Near the creek was large boulders, trees, and bushes. If we could reach the creek in time, we could get the water and take cover before they attacked us. There wasn't time to get water, cross the creek, and run to cover before they cut us down with their carbines.

We had no time to discuss it. Though I was the youngest, they all seemed to look to me to make decisions. I didn't want the job, but someone had to make a decision pronto, so I shouted, "To the creek, boys!"

And off we raced.

We got to the creek and grabbed our canteens. I was about to dismount when I noticed fresh tracks in the mud that sent a shiver up my spine. "Grizzly tracks! Biggest I've ever seen." I'd said it louder than I'd meant to. The others quickly looked around.

Kelby said, "More over here."

"And here. A lot of 'em. Fresh, too," Donnel added.

I said, "Clem and Kelby, give your canteens to Donnel and me. Hold our horses and watch for grizzlies, Henry's gang, redskins, and anyone or anything else that might want to kill us."

Donnel and I filled the canteens, and then we all tied the horses to some brush near the creek bank. The brush shielded 'em from view and maybe bullets but allowed 'em to drink. With our backs to the creek and grizzly tracks, we spread out behind boulders with our 1872 Springfield carbines and what little ammo we had. The damp soil soon seeped through our uniforms. The ripplin' water behind us sounded beautiful. I wondered if it was one of the last sounds I'd ever hear.

Henry and his gang musta spotted us from the hilltop as we was takin' position in the boulders, 'cause they dismounted and began to creep toward us on foot.

I shouted loud enough for my buddies, but not so loud Henry's boys would hear, "Make every shot count, boys. Together, they've got a lot more ammo than we do. We'll be killed if we run out."

They soon started flingin' bullets at us. At first, most weren't comin' very close; but, as they crept closer, their shots got more worrisome. Soon the shots were comin' like drops in a heavy rainstorm, and the noise was so loud I could hardly stand it. The smell of cordite filled the air.

Donnel winged one. That seemed to take the wounded trooper out of the fight. Clem got one, and he didn't get up again. I sure was proud of the four of us. We wasn't wastin' ammo.

We heard the sergeant yellin' orders and organizin' his men. Some fired to keep us pinned down, and some appeared to be tryin' to sneak up on us from our flanks. I shouted to Donnel and

Kelby to watch their sides while Clem and I tried to keep the main group from rushin' us head-on. We killed or wounded three more as Henry's troops moved into position.

Clem yelled, "Donnel's been hit!"

I looked over and saw blood comin' from his head. He'd fallen sideways when he was hit. Donnel's head and part of his body was stickin' out from beside the boulder. Clem looked like he was plannin' to leave his boulder to help Donnel, but some of Henry's men was already usin' Donnel's body for target practice. His body twitched as each bullet hit it. They hit Donnel twice more in the head and at least once in the chest.

I shouted, "Donnel's dead, Clem! You'll be dead, too, if you leave your cover!"

Clem looked poorly but stayed put.

We held 'em off until just shy of pitch dark. We shot two or three more of 'em, but they kept gettin' closer until they was nearly in pistol range.

I heard a noise I didn't recognize comin' from Kelby's position. I turned to see him drop his carbine and grab his neck with both hands as blood gushed out between his fingers. He looked at me with bulgin' eyes and slumped over, not movin' as I saw his blood flow into the creek.

"Kelby took one in the neck. He's gone," I whispered to Clem and gave him time to think on that. Then I said, "I'm down to three rounds. How 'bout you?"

A couple moments later, he answered, "Four."

It was now too dark to see him or much of anything, but I whispered in his direction, "It sure's been good knowin' ya, Clem."

Clem's voice sounded kinda choked up when he answered, "Me, too. Thanks for bein' my friend."

"Likewise."

Suddenly, all hell broke loose. At first, I thought they was all chargin' and firin' at once, but no bullets was bein' flung our way. Then we heard shoutin' and redskin war cries.

I shouted kinda low, "Clem, the redskins musta heard all the shootin' and snuck up on Henry's gang. Let's skedaddle while we can."

We ran for our horses, mounted two, grabbed the reins of the two others, and crossed the creek as fast as we could, countin' on the noise of the battle to cover the noise we made.

We found some cover on t'other side of the creek. It was too dark to see what was happenin', but what we heard was enough to tell the tale. The shootin' soon stopped, and then the only sounds were the whoops and cries of the redskins. We listened longer to try to hear whether the redskins crossed the creek and came after us. We didn't hear horse hooves splashin' and figured we was safe, at least for the time bein'.

Wantin' to put as much distance as we could between us and the redskins and despite the pitch darkness, we kept ridin' in what I hoped was the direction of Prairie Junction. We finally cold camped for 'bout four hours so we could each get a couple of hours sleep while the other stood watch. It was cold and we was exhausted. My eyes kept playin' tricks on me. I kept seein' redskins creepin' up on us, but no one was there.

We rode again at first light. A little before noon, we saw a wagon with an old-timer drivin' it and some purty gals in the back. They was headin' our way, just amblin' along. When the driver saw us, it was like someone lit a fire under him. All of a sudden, he whipped the wagon 'round and raced away.

Figgerin' they might've thought we was redskins or outlaws, we rode after 'em to get closer so they could see we was friendlies. But instead of slowin' down, the driver pulled a pistol, yelled for the girls to get down, and began firin' at us. We didn't expect that, but what happened next surprised us even more. One of the girls hit the old-timer on the head with an iron skillet and pushed him off the wagon.

He banged his head on a big rock. By the way he bounced, I knew he'd be dead by the time he stopped rollin', if he wasn't already.

The wagon was now a runaway and goin' faster than ever. We chased after it and was afraid the wagon would tip over before we could stop it. The women inside was holdin' on for dear life and screamin' like banshees.

The wagon bounced over a large hump. A young woman with long blond hair flew high. She'd have landed on the ground and been hurt badly or killed if the other one hadn't caught and pulled her back into the wagon.

Clem and I galloped on either side of the wagon. The reins bounced along the ground between the scared horses. We reached out to grab the reins at the bridles and hauled back on the bits until the horses slowed down and stopped.

We was all breathin' real hard by the time they did.

The womenfolk climbed down from the wagon, and I saw right away why the driver fired on us. Two crates in the wagon were marked "U.S. Army." Judgin' by their size and length, one was used to hold carbines and the other the ammo for them.

Since they'd been headed toward an area full of hostiles, I figgered they was stolen and the driver was plannin' on sellin' them to the redskins. That musta been why he panicked when he saw us blue-bellies headin' his way. I figgered I'd learn why he'd been hit and throw'd out of the wagon soon enough.

There was two young gals with long blond hair.

The one who clubbed the driver said, "Thank you for rescuing us. I'm Maddy, and this is my sister, Stella."

They was as purty as you please. I was nervous just talkin' to 'em, but answered, "I'm Luke Fernley and this here's Clem. Whatcha doin' way out here so close to redskin country?"

Maddy said, "The driver's name is, well, I guess *was* named Josiah Bleeth. He'd bought some weapons that had been stolen from the army. He said he was going to sell them to the redskins. Bleeth told us it was safe, because he already sold guns to them twice before. He said as long as we were with him, we'd be safe from the Indians."

I took off my hat, scratched an itch on my head, and then asked, "How'd you get tied in with Bleeth?"

"He told our parents he had a teaching job for me in a town named Cottonwood near the

Mexican border. He had official-looking papers and a job description to back up what he said. He even offered to escort me there personally at no charge. I couldn't turn down a good job, not with our parents struggling to feed all our kin and us. Our older brother Jim wanted to make sure everything was honest and offered to come with me to make sure I was all set in my new job."

I said, "That all sounds good."

Maddy replied, "Except it was all lies. Two weeks into the trip…"

Tears appeared in Maddy's eyes, and Stella turned away from us. It took a couple of moments for Maddy to finish the sentence. "Bleeth shot Jim in the back of the head." She sobbed as she added, "Bleeth wouldn't even let us bury him.

"When we got close to a town, he bound and gagged us, and sold Jim's stuff when he went to buy the army guns and ammunition.

"Bleeth came back drunk and told us he'd found men from three different mining camps who wanted to buy us to work as prostitutes. He told all three privately that they had won the auction. Bleeth collected half the money up front from all of them. He bragged that, by the time all three learned he wasn't bringing us to them, he'd be too far away for them to do anything about it. That way he got a lot more money than he would have gotten otherwise. Then he'd take us to another town and do it again.

"We thought about jumping him then, but didn't know where we were, nor where the hostile Indians and outlaw lairs were. We decided to wait until we were near possible help before rebelling. Thank you for showing up when you did."

"Glad we could help. Now what?"

"Would you please take us wherever you're going until we reach civilization and safety? We can try to get home from there."

Clem said to me, "I sure would like to give Donnel and Kelby a proper burial, Luke."

"Me too, Clem. It ain't set right with me that we skedaddled and left 'em unburied. We didn't really have a choice then, but now we have Maddy and Stella to think of."

Maddy offered, "We can help you bury your friends."

"Indians are on the warpath where our friends are."

Maddy didn't let up, saying, "Bleeth was taking us to Indian country before we met you, so what's the difference? I know how to shoot. Our father and brothers taught me. There are lots of guns and ammunition in the wagon. Having one more person who can shoot might make all of us safer."

I changed the subject to buy time to think. "How come you ain't hardly mentioned Stella? You didn't say she got a job offer or could shoot..."

Maddy looked at me, hesitated, and said, "Stella's blind. She wanted to come with me when Bleeth made the offer. We were going to live together in Two Forks."

"I'm sorry, I didn't know."

"That's okay, besides, Stella practiced a lot and can load weapons as fast as sighted people. She can be handy in a fight. Please let us come with you."

Clem and I looked at each other. There was no saying no to Maddy.

"Okay, I won't try to stop you, but there's a good chance none of us will come back alive. And there's somethin' else you need to know." I told how Clem and I came to be deserters.

The ladies talked quietly for a moment, then Maddy turned to me and said, "Thank you for telling us, but it doesn't seem to me that you had any choice. We still want to go with you."

We busted open the crate of carbines. Clem and I each took a second one, and Maddy took two. We cleaned 'em and made sure they fired. Clem and I took as many bullets as we could and still be able to ride fast if we had to. There was enough food and other supplies in the wagon to last us for a week, maybe two. Maddy drove the wagon with Stella as a passenger, while Clem and I rode our own horses, and we ponied Kelby's and Donnel's horses as spares.

Stella cleaned the remainin' carbines in the back of the wagon and loaded them as we rode. Maddy hadn't exaggerated. Stella was as good as anyone at cleanin' and loadin' 'em.

Two nights later and travelin' slow 'cause our horses was tired, we crossed what Clem and I had begun calling Grizzly Creek as quietly as we could.

It didn't take long to find what was left of Donnel and Kelby. The stench was terrible. We shooed away critters and bugs feasting on 'em. It hurt to see our friends like this. I heard Clem sniffle and saw him wipe his eyes and face a time or two. I felt like throwin' up but held it down on account of the womenfolk. Clem and I dug Donnel and Kelby's graves while Maddy stood watch. She didn't flinch from the sights or smells. I never knew women could be so strong.

We said words over them as the sky started to lighten up. We was about to leave when I saw what was left of one of Henry's troopers. He'd almost made it to what had been our tiny defensive line. As the top of the sun peeked into the sky, somethin' glittered near the soldier's nearly naked body.

I walked over to him and saw the redskins had stripped him of everything, includin' the leather pouches he must have been carrying. I'm guessin' they didn't want or need what was inside 'em, so they dumped the contents. Four piles of gold was scattered 'round the trooper.

I called the others to come over. We scooped up the four piles, looked 'round, and found more piles near other bodies. Maddy fetched a shovel from the wagon. It wasn't long before we had 'bout as much gold as we could carry and still ride fast if we had to.

Turned out we didn't have to. The redskins must've moved on after they killed and took what they wanted from Henry's gang and the supply wagon.

We didn't stick 'round waitin' for them to return, and we didn't bury or say words over them that tried to kill us.

We traveled 'til we was near Prairie Junction. Maddy and Stella took the wagon into town and used a little of the gold dust to buy clothes that would fit Clem and me. A lot of gold from the mines and gold fields musta come through the town, 'cause no one seemed to care that the clothes was bought with it.

When they returned, Maddy said, "I wrote a letter to our family, telling them what happened. We also wired some money back home."

Clem and I changed into the new civilian clothes Maddy and Stella brought back with them. We buried anything that was property of the U.S. Army, includin' our names.

We split up the rest of the gold four ways, enough that we wouldn't have money troubles for a long, long time if we didn't go flashin' too much of it anywhere.

Maddy said, "Stella and I talked as we headed back from town. We kind got used to the idea of not needing to live with our parents. We're old enough that we don't need to live at home, and we no longer want to. We love our family, but it's time to leave the nest, and we've already done that. It would feel like going backwards to live with them again. We want to go west. We've heard it's still wide open with a lot of opportunities and room to grow. That suits us fine." She hesitated, looked at Clem and me, and surprised us by sayin', "We'd like to tag along with the two of you for a spell if it's okay with both of you."

I said, "We don't know where we're goin'."

Maddy replied, "That's okay. Neither do we, and we can help protect each others' gold."

That made sense to us. Besides, we liked their company, so we said they could come along. An added bonus was they was easy on the eyes. It felt good to be with them. I was even beginnin' to daydream about Maddy, and it seemed like Clem spent extra time with Stella every chance he got.

Clem drove the wagon into town with Stella riding shotgun. Maddy and I sat in the back.

When we got to town, Maddy smiled, grabbed what appeared to be white papers or envelopes from her stuff, and said she'd be back in a few minutes.

When she returned, she said, "I held off mailing our letter home until now. I wanted to find out whether or not we were heading west with you. I added that information to our letter and said we'd write again when we got to where we were going.

We bought two new horses, more clothes, three Colt Peacemakers and three Winchester repeatin' rifles, plenty of ammo, and other supplies, and headed west.

Well, Bud Bailey, Cord Stewart, and the two young ladies did. We left Clem Tucker and Luke Fernley dead and buried with all the other army stuff. We didn't even bother sayin' words over 'em.

The End

"A Cold, Deadly Ride to Grizzly Creek"

By

'Big' Jim Williams

Chester Goodfield had better days, although today's weather was not hot or cold. But he could feel winter coming. There was even a slight breeze. He heard a few birds chirping and cattle complaining down by the rail yards. The food had been good and the company as good as could be expected, under the circumstances. The shots of redeye after lunch were unexpected.

He wore his favorite wide-brimmed hat. He'd polished his cracked boots for what one man called a *party,* however, not the kind Chester preferred.

He stared down at the growing crowd. He nodded to an old friend, but the man ignored him.

And there was Mrs. Alma Dickey from Boonesfork's general store, a pencil always stuck behind her left ear to update a customer's bill. She'd sold him penny candy when he was a kid. Her drawn face was filled with sadness and tears: hate for Chester, part of a gang that had killed her husband of twenty-seven years the day before, and tears for her shattered dreams. She gave one last look before she wiped her eyes, turned away, and helped by her son, walked away like an old woman for the first time.

Chester cleared his dry throat.

"You wanna say somethin'?" asked the sheriff, another ex-friend. "Ain't got all day."

"Need some water."

The sheriff pressed a canteen to the man's dry mouth.

"Thanks." Chester coughed after several swallows. He looked pale. "I wanna say somethin'... but need to think first."

A minute later, Chester said to the upturned faces, "I'm sorry for what I done as part of 'One-Eyed' Ned Stark's gang. Want you young boys to listen if'n you don't wanna be standin' up here like me someday." He paused. "Don't go robbin' banks, stealin' cattle, or killin'. I'm sorry for what happened, but it ain't gonna bring Mr. Dickey and Jeffrey, his store clerk, back. I stole cattle. Easy money. Then helped robbed that bank in Guthrie. More easy money. Killed a rancher. Didn't mean to. Now I'm gonna meet my maker... or the Devil."

He paused and caught his breath. "Deserve what I'm gittin'." He looked harder at the younger men. "So, don't do what I did, or you'll be standin' up here wishin' you wasn't." He looked at the sheriff. "That's all I wanna say."

The local Baptist minister whispered in Chester's ear. The convicted man lowered his head, listened, nodded, and again turned to the sheriff. "I'm ready," he whispered. "Make the hangman do it right. Don't wanna suffer."

The lawman moved Chester over a trap door and took his hat.

"Keep it," breathed the outlaw. "Paid good money... honest money for it."

A short man with a long white beard moved in. Chester leaned over so the man could pull a hood over his head and tighten the noose's big knot under his left ear. The executioner moved back, stepped to a lever, and nodded toward the sheriff.

The lawman nodded back.

The trapdoor opened, and Chester Goodfield dropped ten feet toward Hell.

*****

A day's ride away, five outlaws rested their lathered horses at a stream at the base of a mountain.

"Damn. Why did Chester kill those people?" asked Dusty McGuire. He drank from his refilled canteen. "No need to do that."

"Chester could never wait for nothin'," complained One-Eyed Ned Stark. "Always wanted things done now. I tried to learn him, but he wouldn't listen." Stark was a six-foot, short-tempered, big-eared man with a barrel chest and bushy eyebrows. A stringed black patch covered a hole where his left eye had been, results of a Union sharpshooter during the recent Civil War.

"Least we got away," said Buck Duncan, a pale-faced seventeen-year-old, the gang's youngest, called Kid by the others, booted from his home by a father more interested in whiskey than a family. He kept looking back toward Boonesfork.

"Bet they've dropped a noose over him by now," predicted Dusty. He was short with a round, pockmarked face.

"Let's git," ordered Stark, "'fore a posse finds us."

They kicked their horses up the pass.

"Ain't got no supplies," complained Squint Blevins, riding behind Stark.

"Then go back to the Dickey store and git some," urged Stark. "Maybe Mrs. Dickey will let you buy on credit."

"We're gonna be danged hungry."

"Or ya could wait and let the posse feed us 'fore they hang us."

The gang also included Dusty McGuire, a tall, gangly man with a dark leathery face and ear-to-ear mustache. Bald Rupert James, although hardly thin enough to cast a shadow, had a beer-belly that did. Both were former cellmates and recent prison escapees.

"We'll stock up in Grizzly Creek on the other side of the mountain," assured Stark, his past filled with bank robberies, cattle rustlings and killings.

"That's a long ride," complained Squint. "What'll we eat between now and then?"

"Chew your nails. Maybe that'll work."

*****

"It's amazing," said Texas Ranger Jake Silverhorn, "how a man like Chester Goodfield could turn outlaw. Dug his own grave when he shot those men in the store." Jake, at six foot two, had shoulder-length hair, a mustache, and carried a Bowie knife. A .44 occupied his right hip.

The eleven-man posse of Rangers and locals led a pack mule loaded with food, blankets, and winter gear. They soon found the outlaws' tracks.

"If we'd been in town," said Ranger Yancy Travis, "we'd have been on 'em like fleas on a dog." Yancy loved playing his harmonica and eating anything that didn't move.

They had been far south of Boonesfork when Jake received word of the shootings.

Although Jake was younger than Yancy, he outranked him in the Rangers because of his leadership and combat experience during The War Between the States, his Yankee past overlooked by Captain Ash Rollins of the Texas Rangers.

The trail led into the mountains, an easy ride until it narrowed into a zigzag climb toward peaks and deep canyons where the posse walked their horses.

"It's got more curves than Blossom Lily at the Mustang Saloon," said Yancy.

"And how would you know that?" smiled Jake, knowing the answer.

"The same way you'd know if you'd do a little scratchin' when you git that special male itch," replied Yancy. "Just climb Blossom's stairs and you'll find paradise."

"And maybe something else doctors can't cure," grinned Jake. "Thought paradise was in Heaven."

"Blossom Lily sure comes close. She's a beauty."

"You sweet on her?"

"I'd marry her if she'd lower her standards, asked me, or had lots of money."

"Not likely," chuckled Jake, "especially the parts about lowering her standards, asking you and having lots of money."

"I'll just have to be content," sighed Yancy, "with chasing outlaws, playin' my harmonica, and seein' Blossom Lily on paydays."

*****

"I see 'em," announced the Kid, peering through Stark's telescope near the mountain's summit. "Men leadin' horses and a pack mule way down there."

"I'll be damned," muttered Stark, taking the scope. "That's Jake Silverhorn leadin'. Thought he was in San Antonio."

"You know him?"

"A Texas Ranger. A good shot, so stay low, Kid." Stark turned and walked up the trail. "They're all yours."

"You're leavin'?"

"You git to kill some Rangers."

"I... I don't wanna kill nobody."

"If they ketch us, you'll hang, too."

"I just held the horses while you robbed the store."

"Makes no difference," huffed Stark. "Being seventeen won't save ya." He tossed a repeating rifle to the Kid. "Ketch up... if you can."

The Kid pleaded as Stark disappeared up the trail. The Kid returned to the ledge, then slid back, stayed low, and moved toward his horse. Two quick shots from above scattered dirt near his boots.

"Git back there, or I'll kill you," yelled Stark, pointing his rifle from beyond the next bend.

The young outlaw reluctantly returned to a protective boulder on the ledge as a cold wind and thick black clouds rolled in from the east. His hands were cold, yet moist and shaking as the first winter snowflakes fell, his bladder suddenly so full he felt pain and quickly relieved himself.

Stark and the other outlaws disappeared over the summit.

"Don't wanna do this," murmured the Kid. Yet he sighted his rifle on the posse as it climbed higher. "I'll fire a round or two to scare 'em." He wiped sweat and snowflakes from his eyes. He gulped water from his canteen to clear his throat. It helped but created another need to relieve himself.

The posse drew closer.

The Kid focused his long gun on the cliff above Jake's head and squeezed off a shot.

Kaplinnng.

The round scattered stone fragments on Jake's head. The Ranger dropped behind his skittish horse and fired toward the rifle's smoke.

Still shaking, the Kid released a second round that nicked a mare's foreleg and wounded a man behind the animal.

"Dammit!" he muttered. "Didn't wanna do that."

He ducked as Jake's multiple rounds chipped his boulder and knocked off his hat. He grabbed it before the wind spun it into the canyon. He returned one quick round, then slid back on fresh snow, raced uphill behind a switchback, and led his horse toward the summit. Several minutes later, he stopped to catch his breath as his facial sweat turned to ice. "Stark left me to get killed so he could get away," spit the Kid, anger and tears in his eyes.

Later, under thicker snow, the exhausted Kid rejoined the riders on the other side of the mountain.

"Did you kill any?" asked Stark.

"Wounded one, but they almost killed me!"

The outlaws laughed, exchanged knowing glances, and left the Kid trailing behind.

*****

"Get down!" yelled Jake, dropping behind the panicked horses and high-kicking mule.

"Up there," pointed Yancy.

Jake grabbed his repeating rifle and laid fire along the high ridge.

"I'm hit!" A posse member gripped his right leg.

Jake zeroed in on what little he could see of the shooter. The snow didn't help. He released a volley that careened off the protective boulder and removed the Kid's hat.

After one more round from the ridge, the firing stopped. When Jake got there the shooter was gone.

"Got a wounded man down here," yelled Yancy, using a tourniquet to stop the bleeding. "Needs a doctor."

One man helped return the wounded rider and horse to Boonesfork. The remaining nine members tightened their winter coats and added rain slickers, as black clouds belched rain and snow. They walked up the trail, their boots slipping and sliding on mud and ice-slick rocks.

"Isn't any shelter around here," shouted Jake to his men. "Maybe find something beyond the summit."

When darkness came, the exhausted men hunkered under a ledge. They munched dried beef, day-old biscuits, shared a can of peaches, and without a fire, got little sleep during the cold night. With dawn they left, anxious to shake life back into their bones.

The posse was left with only seven members when an older man came down with a fever and turned back, aided by his son.

"Where do you think those outlaws are headed?" asked rancher Jacob Musker, related to Boonesfork's dead storeowner.

"Probably Grizzly Creek," predicted Jake. "We'll hang 'em on the trail if we catch 'em."

When they stopped at noon they found enough dry wood to prepare a hot meal of coffee, beans, rice, and steaks from a small beef haunch they'd brought.

"Now you're talkin'," smiled Yancy. "My stomach's as empty as a politician's promises."

More cold wind knifed through their coats as they approached the desert. Jake's hat was tied down, his collar up and buttoned, his numbed feet stuffed in icy boots, his coat sleeve busy wiping his runny nose.

"It's so cold I can't play my harmonica, cuz it'll freeze to my lips," said Yancy.

"Even bad weather has its good points," laughed Jake.

"Ain't been this cold," continued Yancy, "since runnin' to an outhouse in a blizzard."

They sheltered in a windbreak cave with drawings of animals in the soot-blackened walls. "Ancient Indians, judging by the drawings," claimed Jake.

The men collected wood from a downed tree and soon had coffee boiling over a fire. "Nothing smells better than coffee," declared Jake.

"Except Blossom Lily's perfume," winked Yancy.

Tinker Wallace made sourdough biscuits and cooked up a pot of beef and beans, while Yancy briefly played his harmonica.

The men slept on the rocky floor as more snow joined the night.

"Wish the Injuns could have softened these rocks," complained Tinker Wallace, rolling out his blankets. He was short and stocky and related to legendary Ranger Big-Foot Wallace. A scar ran through his left eyebrow, obtained during a fight on the Mississippi when, "I throwed a five-ace gambler overboard to the sharks."

"There ain't no sharks in the Mississippi," declared Yancy.

"Well, somethin' ate him," chuckled Tinker. "Must of been gators."

"Wish them Injuns had left some feather mattresses," added Fuzzy Babcock.

"Leavin' brandy would have been better," said Tinker.

Jake pulled a flask from his boot. "Maybe they did." He took a sip and then looked at his companions. "Want some?"

"Does a horse drink water?" asked Yancy.

"Hot damn!" Ace Pepper slapped his leg.

"Ya don't happen to have Blossom Lily in there, do ya?" asked Yancy.

"Didn't fit."

"Havin' her in my blankets," continued Yancy, "would be better than these rocks."

"Think I might just kiss you," grinned Ace, reaching for Jake's flask.

"Only if you want to lose more teeth. A sip only," emphasized Jake. "Save some for another night."

After drinks, the mood improved as men also enjoyed their tobacco. Fuzzy Babcock, wrapped like a cocoon near the fire, was soon snoring. Ace Pepper smoked his corncob pipe and took the first guard shift.

*****

"What's two covered wagons doin' out here alone?" question One-Eyed Stark. "Easy pickin's. About time we got some food... whiskey... and women."

The Kid didn't like what he heard.

The outlaws waved as they rode toward the snow-dusted wagons.

"Let's suck 'em in, then git what we want," said Stark. "Look like sodbusters. My ol' man was one. All it got him was sunburns, blistered hands, crop-eatin' bugs, a bitchy wife and six hungry kids."

He stopped by the lead wagon, smiled, tipped his hat and adjusted his eye patch. "Where you folks headed?"

"Homesteadin' up north." The bearded driver wore a tattered overcoat, dirty shirt and pants. A rifle rested across his lap. "Farmers. Left Grizzly Creek 'bout a week ago."

A blanket-wrapped wife and three kids walked alongside. One was a tall girl fast becoming a woman. Her blue eyes sparkled beneath a sunbonnet that revealed long yellow hair. She smiled when her eyes met the Kid's.

Stark stared at the girl's developing body.

The driver cocked his rifle.

An older man stood by the driver on the opposite side of the wagon, the hammers pulled back on his shotgun. They were brothers, they said.

"Got any water to spare?" asked Stark. "Just came through those dry mountains."

"See lots of snow up there," said the first driver.

"Too cold to melt."

"Can spare a little," said the older traveler. "We got a long way to go."

"Glory be to God." Stark raised his arms like a Sunday preacher. "We thank you good Samaritans for helpin' strangers like the Bible says. We'll welcome whatever you can spare." He again smiled.

The men didn't smile back.

"Kid," ordered Stark, "fill our canteens. Then," he whispered, "git out of the way."

The Kid moved to the wagon's water barrel.

The older man came around, lifted the barrel's lid, stepped back, but kept his eyes on the riders, his finger on his scattergun's trigger.

"Don't think he trusts us," whispered Squint.

"A downright shame," replied Stark, "since we're God-fearin' folks."

The Kid spilled water when the young girl smiled in his direction.

"Careful, boy!" warned the second man. "That water's precious. And, Joella," he said to the girl, "go help yer ma."

Stark's eyes followed Joella's body as she hurried to the second wagon where an older woman and two kids peered from inside.

"I'm sorry, sir," said the Kid. "I didn't—"

He never finished his apology before the four mounted outlaws—at a nod from Stark—drew sidearms and killed the two men. The Kid rolled under the wagon and then yelled, "What did you do that for?"

The women screamed and raced to their husbands.

Within seconds, the only one Stark left alive was Joella.

"Hate sodbusters!" spit Stark.

He notched his pistol's grip, one notch for each adult, half notches for the kids.

*****

Jake saw smoke on the snowy horizon. "A couple of burning prairie schooners," he said, focusing binoculars. "Hope it's not what I think."

"What?" asked Yancy.

"One-Eyed Ned Stark," sighed Jake. "There's nothing that soulless killer wouldn't do."

The wagons were smoldering, boxes ripped opened, furniture and farm implements scattered among the bodies of men, women and children.

"I *hate* Ned Stark and every man who rides with him," said Jake, pale and shaking. "God may forgive them, but I won't!"

They wrapped the victims in salvaged clothes and canvas and began digging graves. "We don't even know their names," said a teary Fuzzy Babcock, making crosses.

A foot into digging, Yancy stopped. "I hear somethin'," he said, "like someone's cryin'."

Every man stopped digging and listened.

"Coming from over there." Jake raced toward an arroyo yards away, stopped at the edge, ripped off his coat and jumped down.

Joella was nude, curled into a dirty, whimpering ball, her hair disheveled, her face bruised and bloody. She screamed when Jake placed his coat over her shaking body. "No, no, not again," she pleaded, gushing tears. "Please, not again."

Jake spoke softly and gently. "We're Texas Rangers. You're safe now. The killers are gone. We'll protect you."

She continued to cry and shake as Jake repeated his words. He talked until Joella finally realized she was safe, let Jake pick her up, and wrap her in blankets by a fire away from the graves.

That's when Jake downed the last of his brandy.

"What'd they do to her?" asked Yancy.

"Guess!" Jake wiped his eyes. "Her name's Joella. She heard Stark say they're heading to

Grizzly Creek. Need to splint her right arm. They broke it. Surprised she's still alive."

After the burials, they rode out, leaving Ace and Fuzzy to get Joella to the doctor in Grizzly Creek when she could ride.

*****

"Why did you have to kill those folks?" pleaded the Kid, his head in a bloodied bandage. "Then rape and kill the girl?"

He tried to save Joella, but was knocked unconscious, pistol-whipped by the outlaw.

"Been a long time since I had somethin' that young and good lookin'... without buyin' it."

The Kid wiped his eyes, muttered, and staggered toward his horse.

"What'd you say, Kid?" commanded Stark.

"I'm leavin'."

"Not till I say you're leavin'."

"Can't take this no more."

"You're weak. Knowed it the first time I saw you."

The Kid slumped in the saddle. "You gonna shoot me in the back?"

"You'll be the first to know."

A heavier storm was coming as the Kid nudged his horse east toward Grizzly Creek.

Stark drew his sidearm.

"Let him go." Splint put his hand on the outlaw's arm, "So he can tell the world One-Eyed Ned Stark is the most feared outlaw in the West. He'll help make ya famous."

Stark grinned. "Yeah, why not," he said. "I'd like bein' famous. I'll just scare him." He squinted with his one eye, fired several close rounds and laughed as the Kid's startled horse broke into a gallop. "Now, I feel better. Let's take what we want, burn the wagons, and head for Grizzly Creek, cuz there's a bank there that needs robbin'."

"That's a long ride," stated Splint.

"You know any other way to git there?"

"No..."

"Then shut up."

The outlaws wrapped themselves in the sodbusters' quilts and blankets. The desert was cold during the day and colder at night.

Three days later Splint said, "Thought it was an easy ride to Grizzly Creek."

"Was till we got lost in that whiteout," replied Stark.

"We're runnin' out of food. Them sodbusters didn't carry much."

Stomachs got emptier before Stark shot a rabbit, and Dusty found a frozen rattler.

"Ain't never ate no snake," said Splint, "but will now, I reckon."

"Hold the head in one hand, the tail in the other," chuckled Stark, "and eat it like corn on the cob. The fangs make good toothpicks."

Stark skinned the six-foot viper while the others scrounged for wood to build a fire. They spent the cold night out of the wind in a dry creek bed.

"My horse is about played out," revealed Dusty, leading the limping animal. "She ain't gonna make it. Maybe we should double back. Find someplace warm."

"Go ahead and say *Hello* to Jake Silverhorn and his posse. Bet he's still trackin' us. He never gives up. Take a rope so he can hang ya like Chester Goodfield."

The four had ridden themselves and their horses to exhaustion. They were out of food, water and patience and decided the time had come to quit running, take a stand, and rob the Grizzly Creek Bank.

They killed and ate part of Dusty's mare two days before staggering through snow into Grizzly Creek.

"Wearin' the same stinkin' clothes for over a week won't git me a good-lookin' whore," said Splint, sniffing himself.

"No woman's gonna let you touch her even for a hundred dollars," chuckled Stark.

"The way I smell, I wouldn't touch me for a hundred dollars."

*****

The outlaws left their surviving horses at the Grizzly Creek Livery, stuffed themselves at a restaurant and got drunk. They bought clothes and bathed at the barbershop. "Check out the bank tomorrow," said Stark. "Now, all I wanna do is sleep in a warm hotel room."

A mile away, the Kid camped in a grove of trees and thought about Joella, not knowing she was alive. Eating rabbits and riding ahead of the storm had saved his life.

*****

Stark entered the bank and talked to a teller about opening an account.

Squint, pretending to write at a tall table, studied the big guard at the front door. *He ain't gonna be easy to take,* he thought. *Think I saw him years back wearing a badge.* Squint left after Stark did.

"Excuse me, sir," said the guard. "You look familiar. You from around here?"

"Just passin' through," replied Squint.

"Come again when we ain't so busy."

Stark and Squint joined Dusty McGuire and Rupert James at a saloon's back table.

"The guard carries a shotgun and pistol," said Squint. "Think he's an ex-lawman. Looked me over real good. Maybe saw one of my wanted posters."

"Friday's payday at the mines," confirmed Stark. "The bank'll be loaded. We'll walk in early, grab the money, kill the guard and ride out."

"Sounds too easy," complained Dusty. "Things never go perfect."

"Ya don't think we should rob the bank?"

"Bein' cautious has kept me alive, and I wanna keep it that way."

"We'll hit 'em Friday," continued Stark.

*****

The posse reached Grizzly Creek later that day minus two cattlemen who left, saying, "We've got ranches to run." Their departure left only Jake, Yancy, Ace Pepper, Fuzzy Babcock, and Tinker Wallace.

"Stark's here someplace," said Jake. "Joella heard them talking about robbing the bank."

"There it is." Yancy nodded across the street.

Jake and Yancy showed their Ranger badges and met with the bank manager behind closed doors.

"Got the big monthly payroll for the mines comin' Friday," revealed the manager.

"That's when they'll strike," predicted Jake. "We'll be ready."

* * *

The following day, Ace Pepper and Fuzzy Babcock brought Joella into the doctor's office in Grizzly Creek.

"Animals," said the doctor, bandaging the young girl and putting a cast on her arm. The doctor's wife took Joella, who refused to talk, into a quiet back room.

"Worse than animals," said Ace. "Hope your town marshal can do somethin'."

"He won't be helpin'," said the doctor.

"Why not?"

"Died last week."

*****

Two days later at ten-fifteen a.m., the outlaws entered the bank. Outside, Dusty McGuire lit a cigar, readjusted his gun belt, and leaned against a wall near the entrance. He pretended to read a newspaper, although he couldn't read or write.

Stark, Squint and Rupert James entered the bank.

Stark carried a carpetbag and walked to a teller's cage. "Spoke with you a couple of days ago," he said, placing the bag on the counter.

"Yes, sir. Can't forgit a man wearin' an eye patch," he said.

"You sure my money's gonna be safe in your bank?" Stark patted his bag.

"Absolutely. We've never been robbed." The clerk indicated the guard at the door.

Rupert waited in line for the second teller.

Squint stood on the opposite side of the same waist-high table—it would offer some protection, if needed—and again pretended to write, although he also couldn't read or write.

Stark put his hand inside his carpetbag and whispered to the teller, "I have a double-barreled, sawed-off shotgun in here. Yell for help and I'll blow your head off. Do you understand?"

The man nodded.

"Good," said Stark. "You armed?"

"No... No, sir."

"If you're lyin', I'll kill you."

"Ain't lyin'," breathed the teller.

"Where's the payroll money for the mines?"

"Over... there." The teller didn't turn his head, only his eyes toward the slightly open walk-in vault. A drop of sweat suddenly glistened above his left eyebrow.

Stark nodded to Squint, who casually followed him behind the teller's cage, drew his sidearm, and moved toward the vault. Stark pulled the shotgun from the bag, ordered the teller onto the floor, and tossed the bag to Squint. "Fill it," he whispered, "while I kill the guard."

Rupert, at the second cage, shielded his pistol and quietly ordered the teller to empty his cash drawer into a sack he shoved forward.

Stark, crouched behind his teller's cage, raised his shotgun and eyed the frowning guard by the front door who thought: *Where's the teller, and what are those two strangers doing behind the counter?*

Squint opened the vault door and heard, "Drop your gun or I'll shoot!" It was Jake Silverhorn.

Squint didn't.

Jake's two shots knocked Squint against Stark, who, off balance, triggered one round into the floor, sending splinters and pellets toward Jake. Jake fired at Stark as the outlaw leaped over the counter, grabbed an elderly woman as a shield and fired his second shotgun barrel, removing half the front window, as the guard dived behind a desk, but held fire to avoid hitting the woman.

Stark dropped the shotgun, pulled his pistol and fired a round that ripped through the desk into the guard's left arm.

Before Rupert could grab the second teller's money sack, Yancy Travis exited the manager's office and ordered the outlaw to drop his weapon. Rupert clutched the sack with his left hand and fired with his right. The bullet missed Yancy but shattered the manager's glass door.

Ranger Ace Pepper, masquerading at a desk behind the counter, fired his pistol, piercing the bag and scattering the money, but missed Squint.

Jake jumped the counter and tackled Stark, freeing the woman. Ranger and outlaw rolled across the floor, each man gripping the other's gun hand. Stark tried to rip free but couldn't. They knocked over a fake potted palm and rolled farther before Jake slammed a knee into the outlaw's groin.

Rupert ducked, fired, but missed Ace Pepper behind the counter, as Yancy shot the outlaw in his left side. Rupert staggered toward the front door where the bank guard cut him in half with a shotgun blast.

Dusty McGuire, outside the bank, fired through what little remained of the window, sending glass shards into the guard's back. Fire from the guard's second barrel slammed Dusty against a lamppost.

Jake ripped the handgun from Stark and got to his feet. The outlaw cursed, rolled onto his side. Then, with one swift kick, knocked Jake's legs out from under him, and raced toward the door. The guard, reloading, was knocked to the floor as Stark slammed into him and fled. Outside he used Dusty as a shield as he dragged him down the street.

Posse members Fuzzy Babcock and Tinker Wallace, posted outside, fired at Stark.

Jake's shot dropped Dusty as Stark pushed several people aside, ripped a child from its mother's arms, and jumped on a horse. Jake held fire as the killer raced around a freight wagon, dropped the kid, and left Grizzly Creek as the frantic mother ran toward her crying child.

Two witnesses from across the street at a second floor window wished they could have shot Stark. It was Joella and ex-gang member, Buck Duncan, better known as the Kid.

Jake galloped after Stark into the desert, letting his horse run free as he used both hands to release round after rifle round at Stark, who twisted in the saddle, pulled his long gun and fired, as Jake slowly closed the gap on the snowy plain.

Jake took his time aiming and winged the outlaw. One more round and he knocked Stark from his saddle. The outlaw landed on his right side and rolled into sagebrush, ending face down against a boulder. He was bleeding from his back, right shoulder and head. After several attempts, he slowly twisted onto his back. His eye patch dangled from a snowy bush, revealing a deep hole where his left eye had been.

Jake dismounted and grabbed the killer's sidearm.

Stark slowly struggled into a sitting position against the boulder and wiped dirt and blood from his eyes with his right hand. His left arm dangled at his side. "You broke my arm," he moaned.

"Good," replied Jake. "It's a beginning."

Stark coughed, spit dirt, and begged for water.

"Not wasting a drop on your worthless hide," growled Jake.

"You'd... deny a dyin' man... water?"

Jake put the muzzle of his rifle against Stark's head. "You're damned lucky I don't put a bullet in you for what you did in Boonesfork and to those two wagon families."

"Go ahead," challenged the killer.

"Nope. Gonna let you bleed out."

"A good Christian... won't give a dyin'... man water."

"Not for what you did to Joella."

"I didn't do nothin'. It was—"

"She tells a different story," interrupted Jake.

"What?"

"She's alive in Grizzly Creek."

"She's lyin'. I... tried... to save her," pleaded Stark. "It was—"

"All of you raped her, she said."

"She's lyin'. I told 'em not to."

"Now's the time to ask God for forgiveness," urged Jake, "because you're dying. But I don't expect it from a killer like you."

Stark grabbed his boots to keep from falling back. "I'd do it all over again if I could."

"That's the only honest thing you've ever said."

"You ain't no better," coughed the killer, "denyin' a dyin' man... water. If there's a God, he'll write that... in his big book."

Jake shrugged, lowered his weapon, turned and walked toward his horse and canteen. Then heard...

Click.

...from behind.

He spun as Stark pulled a derringer from his right boot.

Jake lifted his rifle.

Stark lifted his pistol.

Both fired.

Jake put a .44 slug into Stark's chest as the outlaw's shot whistled past Jake's left ear. Smoke drifted from the derringer as the killer slumped against the boulder and slowly slid onto the ground, his one good eye half-closed in death.

*****

In Grizzly Creek, Jake spoke with Joella's doctor.

"She's tough," said the doctor. "Her bruises look better. Her arm's healin' nicely. And she's met a young man who's helpin' her through all this."

"His name's Buck Duncan," smiled the doctor's wife. "She calls him Kid. *Love* has a way of curin' many ills." She smiled at her husband. "They're goin' west when Joella's well. Maybe California."

*****

339

"No need to arrest the Kid," confided Jake to Yancy as the small posse left Grizzly Creek. "Told me he was the shooter in the mountains."

"But he wounded one of our men," frowned Yancy.

"Let's give him a second chance. He's through with outlawing. Proved that at the wagons. Now he's got a beautiful young gal in his life. Won't tell anyone he rode with One-Eyed Ned Stark."

"The Kid became a man when he tried to defend Joella," continued Yancy, "then help care for her."

"Love can do that," said Jake.

"How would you know?"

"Been there a time or two."

"You're full of surprises, Jake. But that's not the only thing you're full of," laughed Yancy, spurring his horse ahead.

It was a long ride back to Boonesfork.

Jake kept Stark's eye patch, derringer and notched pistol.

The End

Scott Harris

Mac Guidry

By

Special Guest Author

As I looked out past the rocks that sheltered me, a shiver flowed through me and it wasn't even cold weather yet. I'm Michael Anthony Charles Guidry, Mac for short. And I'm ten years old.

The five of us, four men and a boy, rode our horses near to them collapsin'. We were out of food, had little water, and Pa had no patience left. He decided it was time to quit runnin' and take a stand.

We rode into this bunch of big rocks and trees at the mouth of a canyon. Pa, George Washington Guidry, was the first off his horse. I saw him stagger a little when his feet hit the ground.

My pa never staggered, so I knew something was wrong. Something real bad.

Isaac came in next, Moses after him, then Joshua right before me. At the time, that struck me as funny in an odd way. That was the order of our births, too.

I was not only the youngest, but also different from the others. My ma was Spanish, so where all of my brothers and my pa were dark as midnight, I was sorta the color of coffee with cream in it.

But that didn't make any difference to the men who were chasing us. Mason Ritter's men. Not his cowboys, his hired guns.

We let the horses go, knowin' as tired as they were, they wouldn't go far.

When I got down off my horse, I saw Pa leaning against his. Blood stained the shirt he wore and the left leg of his pants. Gingerly, he pulled open his shirt, revealin' a hole in his side just above his belt. I rushed over to him.

"Pa! You're hurt!"

"Shoot, boy. I've hurt myself worse shavin'." He laid a hand on top of my head and shook it a little. Then he pushed his shirt tail into the hole to stop the bleeding. "Help me get more of this shirt tail in the hole in my back."

I tried not to hurt him as I wadded up the shirt tail and shoved it in the hole. It was hard to see the hole through the tears that welled up in my eyes. Pa took over.

"Don't worry none about hurtin' me, Mac. You ain't gonna hurt me near as much as that bullet did."

Pa glanced out over the rocks. "I don't see none of those men yet. Reckon we got out ahead of 'em some. That'll give us time to get ready." He walked over to Isaac. "How bad are you hit, son?"

Isaac lay in the tiny shade behind a boulder. "Can't move my left arm, Pa. They got me real good in the shoulder."

Pa didn't say anything as he examined Isaac's shoulder. "Good thing you're right handed, then."

Both of them grinned at that.

"Boys," Pa raised his voice as only he could so we all would hear him. "Our horses are wore plumb out, so I don't think we're goin' any farther than this. Get yourselves ready. Those men of Ritter's will be here before long. We need to let 'em know who they're facin'."

I watched the others get themselves ready. Pa glanced over at me once. That's when I hunkered down behind this rock. And my thoughts roamed back to seven months ago when most of the worst from Ritter started.

*****

Seven months ago, me and Pa were getting the spring wagon ready for a trip to Cade's Crossing. That was the nearest town, about twenty miles from our place.

My ma, Consuela, caught lung fever from bein' out in the cold rain, looking for a runaway horse.

348

"We done tried ever'thing your mama could think of," Pa said as we hitched up the team to the wagon. I think he was talking because he was worried. "And ever'thing I could remember my mama tellin' me about doctorin' people." He shook his head and frowned. "Nothin's worked. So, now we gotta go see if the doctor will come out or at least give us some medicine for her."

I stopped what I was doin' and looked at Pa. I felt my forehead wrinkle up like it does when I'm trying to figure somethin' out. "But, Pa, what about what Mr. Ritter said?"

Ritter had spread the word in Cade's Crossing that nobody was to sell us anything unless we had cash money. That pretty much meant we couldn't buy nothin'.

"Don't matter," he said, a determined expression on his face. "We gotta get some help for your mama."

After we finished gettin' the team hitched, we climbed up on the hard wood wagon seat and set off. I hadn't seen Pa go into town wearin' his pistol before. Usually all we had with us was the double-barrel shotgun layin' under the seat.

Seein' that pistol made me realize we were goin' into territory where nobody liked us. I don't mind sayin' I was scared.

The whole way into town neither of us said anything. Pa kept his eyes moving along both sides of the trail and even behind us at times.

There was one point where the trail into town passed close to Ritter's land. I saw a cowboy settin' on his horse, watchin' over some cows as they watered at a little stream. As soon as he caught sight of us, he reined his horse around and galloped hard over the hill toward Ritter's main ranch house.

We watched the man until he rode out of sight over the hill. Then Pa said, "I reckon Mr. Ritter will be ready for us when we get to town."

Two hours later we rolled down the short main street of Cade's Crossing. The community got its name from the shallow spot on the Green River that was the only place in miles to cross without gettin' totally wet. Nobody knew who Cade had been.

At the opposite end of town, the doctor's home and office were in a white clapboard house with a little fence around it. Pa pulled the team to a stop in front of the house. He handed the reins to me and said, "Stay here."

Pa didn't even get to the porch before the door opened and the doctor stood there. "George, you know I can't help you."

"But, Doc, Consuela ain't no better. Her fever is real high. You've got to do something! At least give me some medicine for her."

"I'd really like to, George. Really, I would." The doctor glanced up and down the street. Then he leaned over real close to Pa and said in a low voice, "Morgan Ritter told me not to have anything to do with you. So, I can't help you." He stepped back, turning to go inside. Then, almost in a whisper, the doctor said over his shoulder, "If you can get some laudanum, that might help."

Pa came back to the wagon real fast. He turned the team around in the street and headed back to the only general store in town. He stopped in front of the store and climbed down.

"Wait for me," he told me. "I'll be back in a minute."

Soon as Pa went into the store, I looked down the street and saw three men ridin' in quick-like. When they got closer, I saw it was Morgan Ritter and two men. They rode right up to the wagon where I sat. I was so scared, I almost peed my pants.

The three of 'em just pulled their horses to a stop and stared at me. Morgan Ritter was the biggest rancher in the area. His physical size matched the size of his land and almost matched the size of his greed. One of the men with him worked for him. I'd seen him ridin' with Ritter before.

The other man was a stranger. A stranger wearing a tied-down gun, dressed all in black. Even his eyes were black and looked dead.

"Where's your pa, boy?" Ritter's voice sounded like barbed wire dragged through an iron pipe.

I pointed to the store and managed to get out, "He, he's in there."

Right then, Pa stepped out on the wooden boardwalk in front of the store. I remember his boots sounded like thunder on the walk. "I'm right here, Mr. Ritter."

"George, I told you nobody in this town will sell anything to you unless you have cash money." He shifted in his saddle. "Do you have cash money?"

"You know I don't, Mr. Ritter. But my wife, she's real sick. I gotta have medicine for her." Pa swallowed hard. "She may die if she don't get medicine."

Ritter glanced from one of the men with him to the other, then back to Pa. With a tiny laugh, he said, "Well, that's what she gets for marryin' a n—"

"DON'T SAY IT, MR. RITTER!" I'd never heard my pa say anything in that kind of voice before.

"All right, George. I won't say it."

"But I will." The man all in black dismounted. He was grinnin' the entire time.

Pa turned slightly to face the man. "When you do, mister, you better draw at the same time."

"All right." The man went for his gun.

Later, I couldn't remember seein' Pa draw his pistol. But he did and shot that man right in the chest. The man's pistol went off into the ground.

Everyone froze.

I'd never seen Pa shoot a pistol before. I just sat there on that hard wooden wagon seat with my mouth open.

Slowly, Pa turned to stare at Ritter. That rancher turned pale when he caught the expression on Pa's face. His eyes flitted from the pistol in Pa's hand to the hardness around his eyes.

"I wish you hadn't made me do that, Ritter," Pa said in a low voice. "I didn't want my son to see this kind of thing."

Ritter straightened up in his saddle. "How did I make you do that, George?"

"You brought a gunfighter into this disagreement between us." Pa slowly ejected the empty shell from his pistol and replaced it with a live round from his belt. He never took his eyes off Ritter or the other man with him.

"What's goin' on here?" came an authoritative voice from behind the mounted men.

Neither Pa nor Ritter said anything at first. Even I understood this was a dangerous time for Pa. If Ritter accused him of murderin' that man in black, he would be believed. No one would say anything against him.

"George was havin' words with Ritter, Marshal." The voice from behind Pa was that of Westerman, the storekeeper. "Then this feller," he pointed to the dead gunfighter, "braced George. It was a fair fight. George got him fair and square." The man sounded like he actually admired Pa for what he did.

The marshal glanced from Pa to the dead man. Then he turned his face to gaze up at Ritter. "That the way it happened, Mr. Ritter?"

After a few seconds while he stared at Pa, Ritter responded, "Yeah, Marshal. That's the way it happened." Then he reined his horse around and rode back toward his ranch, the man with him following.

"I'm gonna have to have your gun, George." The marshal held out a hand.

"What for? You heard what they both said. It was a fair fight."

"I'll need it for evidence in case somethin' else comes up in connection with this gunplay."

I watched Pa put his hand on the butt of his pistol. That hardness that was in his eyes before came back. "If you need it for evidence later, you know where you can come and get it."

Never taking his eyes off the marshal, Pa climbed back onto the wagon seat. He never did take his hand off the butt of that pistol.

"Take us home, son," he said in that soft way of talkin' Pa had.

Once they were out of town, Pa seemed to relax. He took the reins from me. For a time after that, we rode without talkin'.

Finally, I couldn't keep it in. "I never saw you shoot like that, Pa. Where did you learn how?"

Pa took a few seconds before he replied. "A black man has to learn a lot of things to survive, son. Shootin' a pistol was one of the things I learned."

"Is that the first man you've shot, Pa?"

Pa sighed real big. "No, Mac, it ain't. But I hope it's the last." Another sigh. "But I don't think it will be."

We were both quiet again for a while. Then, "Pa, did you get any medicine for Ma?"

"No, son." I heard somethin' in his voice I hadn't heard before. Later, I found out it was dejection and hopelessness.

After a few more minutes, I asked, "Why do that hate us, Pa?"

"I don't think all of 'em hate us, Mac. Yeah, there are some who do, but most of 'em are just afraid of Ritter. Afraid he'll take his business someplace else and not buy from them. When you look at how much he spends and how much we spend, I can understand that a little. Some of 'em follow him 'cause he's a big man with lots of land and cattle. It makes them feel bigger to follow him. Some of 'em hate us because we're black. They can't get over the fact that the Civil War ended twenty years ago. They think ever'body with our color skin should still be slaves."

I chewed on that for a couple of minutes. "Ritter hates us, Pa. Why does he hate us?"

"I don't think Ritter hates us, Mac. I think he just wants the land and water we have." He glanced over at me. "You remember he didn't even bother to speak to us 'til we dug that well and struck so much water. Then he took notice. Tried to buy the ranch, but I wouldn't sell, no matter how much he offered. Now, he's gonna do whatever he can to get that water from us."

"A lot of folks don't like that you married Ma. I heard some in town say it ain't natural for a black man to marry a white woman."

This time I could hear the sadness in Pa's voice real clear. "You know your mama ain't white, she's Spanish. From down in Mexico. I know there are some who said what you heard, but those folks are just ignorant." He focused then on the trail ahead of us. "You take the reins again, Mac."

I followed his gaze out in front of us. "What is it, Pa? Trouble?"

"I don't know, Mac. Somebody's raisin' a whole lot of dust ridin' toward us. I can't make out who it is yet." He studied that dust cloud that kept on comin' for another long minute. "Whoever it is rides just like Isaac. And he's ridin' a black horse like Isaac favors." Another few seconds, watchin' the rider. "It is Isaac!" A long pause. I saw Pa's shoulders slump. "I think he's bringin' bad news, son."

In another minute, Isaac pulled his lathered black horse to a stop beside our wagon. "Pa! Consuela's..."

Isaac couldn't finish, so Pa did for him. "She's gone, ain't she?"

All Isaac could manage through his tears was a nod. "I'm sorry, Pa," he finally managed to get out.

I felt my own tears rollin' down my cheeks. I heard Pa say, "That's all right, son." I didn't know if he was talking to me or to Isaac. Pa's strong arm went around my shoulder, and I leaned into him as I cried.

"No need to ruin a good horse by runnin' him back now," Pa said to Isaac. "You just ride along with us. Consuela ain't hurtin' no more now."

The next couple of days blurred by. No one bothered to come by the ranch and say anything. Pa cleaned Ma up, and I suspected he mourned her in his own way. Isaac and the other two boys build a real good coffin for her. We all helped lay her down in it.

Closin' my ma in that coffin really bothered me.

"Boys," Pa said to us that night. "I'm takin' Consuela down to Mexico to her family. I want you boys to stay right here while I'm gone. Don't go ridin' out anywhere, just stay right here."

"I'm goin', too, Pa." I'd decided that right then.

Pa looked me over for a long time. I did my best to show him I was goin'. "I expect if I tell you no, you'll just follow me anyway, won't you?"

"Yes, sir." I glanced around at my three brothers. "And none of my brothers can stop me."

"I reckon I better let you go, then. C'mere." He grabbed me and pulled me into his arms. "You got the best of me and your mama both." Pa let me go and turned away with a sniff.

After tellin' the other boys we'd be back in three, four days, me'n Pa climbed onto the wagon seat and set off. The trip went by fast. If there hadn't been trouble at home, Pa said we would've stayed longer. But he was worried about the other boys.

And his worry was real.

Late the third day when it was comin' on night, Pa pulled the wagon onto that little hill that overlooked the ranch buildings. He hauled back on the reins, stoppin' us right there.

For a few minutes, we just sat there, both of us lookin' over the ranch below. The light was real low and fadin' fast.

"Somethin's wrong, ain't it, Pa?" I flicked my gaze from the buildings down below to Pa's face, then back again.

"Yeah, there is. Ain't no lights in the house down there." A brief pause. "There's somethin' wrong with the barn, too."

We studied those buildings down below us for several more minutes. Pa even looked at the trees and open area around the ranch.

"Let's go down there and see what's goin' on," Pa said then. "You take the reins." He pulled the shotgun out from under the seat.

I just stared at that shotgun for a few seconds. I don't know why, but it scared me. Never had before, but it did that time.

"Come on, son," Pa said in that soft voice. "Get us on down there."

I started the horses out at a walk, holding the reins tight, so they wouldn't speed up when they sensed home comin' close. As we got closer, I could see what was wrong with the barn.

One side of it had been burned.

When we rolled into the ranch yard, the front door of the house opened, and my brothers walked out. My middle brother, Moses, wore a white bandage around his head.

I stopped the team, and Pa climbed down. The other boys stepped down off the porch.

Pa walked up close to Moses and looked over the bandage. "What happened?" he asked my brothers as a group.

"Some of Ritter's men paid us a visit," Isaac reported. "Two nights ago, right after dark. They came in yellin' and shootin' in the air, like they was gonna scare us. Tried to set the barn on fire, but none of those boys could start a fire worth spit." He laid a hand on Moses' shoulder. "This 'un ran out on the porch and started shootin'. That's how he got this little scratch. We been keepin' a guard out ever' night since."

Pa faced Moses. "Tell me you hit one of 'em at least."

Moses grinned. "I did, Pa. Knocked him out of the saddle, but them others put him back on his horse and lit out. You should'a seen 'em run!"

"Did y'all go to the marshal or sheriff?"

"No, Pa. You told us not to leave the ranch."

"Yeah, I did. All right, I'll go into town and see the marshal tomorrow." He glanced over at the barn. "Did that fire do much damage?"

"No. Just burned some boards on the outside, then it went out by itself." Isaac grinned. "Like I said, those boys can't build fires. They should've tossed one of their torches inside into the hay."

"Well, we need to get some sleep. Might be some nights when we don't get much. You boys got anything left from supper?"

The next mornin' before Pa could even get his horse saddled to go into Cade's Crossing, Sheriff Jake Latrone rode into the ranch yard. Three men rode with him, one of them was the same man of Ritter's who was with him when Pa shot the gunfighter.

I was in the barn with Pa when we heard their horses walkin' in the yard. Pa slipped the thong off the hammer of the pistol he wore. He stepped out of the barn with me right behind him. "Howdy, Sheriff."

Latrone and the three men with him had been lookin' at the house, so he was behind them. All of them started when he spoke.

They whirled their horses around, their hands going to the pistols they wore.

Pa smiled. "You don't need your pistols, Sheriff."

"You never know when you're after criminals, George," the sheriff replied. None of the men took their hands from their pistols.

"My boys are gettin' nervous, Sheriff." He nodded toward the house. "I might not be able to control 'em much longer."

The sheriff looked over his shoulder, saw my three brothers at one of the windows and both corners of the house, holding rifles pointed at him and the others. He swallowed aloud, then said to the others, "It's all right, boys. You can relax."

Once the men took their hands off their guns, Pa waved his hand, and my brothers lowered their rifles. "Now, Sheriff, what can I do for you? You said somethin' about bein' after criminals."

"Uh, yeah, yeah, that's right. We're here for your boy, Moses. He shot one of Mr. Ritter's men for no reason." He glanced back at my brothers behind him. "Which one's Moses?"

"You don't have to worry about which one is Moses, Sheriff. He shot a man who was here shootin' at him and his brothers and tryin' to burn down my barn." Pa narrowed his eyes and glanced from the sheriff to Ritter's man. "And anybody who says different is a damn liar."

"Why, you damn n—"

Pa stopped Ritter's man in mid-sentence. "You better not say what you were goin' to say, mister.

If you do, you'n me are gonna have some for-real problems."

Ritter's man glared at Pa for a few seconds, then he eased back down in his saddle. Slowly, he put his hands on his saddle horn.

"Now, Sheriff, you said you want to arrest Moses. Well, that ain't gonna happen. You can see he was wounded in that attack. And you can see the barn's been burned. My boys were home, and someone came in the night to burn us out. The only one who wants this land and has been willin' to do whatever he could to get it is Ritter. If you want to arrest somebody, go arrest him."

The sheriff squirmed in his saddle. "Now, you know I can't do that. He's Morgan Ritter!"

If there had ever been any doubt that Ritter owned the sheriff, it was gone now.

"He's gonna be awful mad that you didn't let me arrest your boy, George." The sheriff frowned and reined his horse around. The other men followed him, Ritter's man the last one to leave.

Pa watched as the men rode out of sight. Then, he turned to us. "Boys, it's gonna get serious now."

That night, it did.

To be on the safe side, Pa kept all of us boys on guard all night. He was sure Ritter would attack again.

It was after midnight when they came. Quietly this time.

Pa caught a movement out of the corner of his eye. He gripped my shoulder as I stood beside him He stood at the end of the porch, hidden by the corner of the house.

Three of them ran lightly across the ranch yard toward the barn. Moses signaled that he saw them, too. He ran across the yard in the shadows and circled around to the back of the barn. In another minute, three shots rang out from there.

Those shots were the opening salvo of the battle. From three sides, rifle fire sent bullets whining through the air, hitting the sides of the house and barn, kicking up dirt as they hit in the space between the house and the barn.

Pa and all of his boys, including me, returned fire, aiming at the winks of muzzle blasts they could see. Every once in a while, a scream of pain came from one of the men who got hit.

Isaac was one of those hit. With a grunt of pain, he grabbed his shoulder.

"How bad you hit?" Pa called out.

"Just my shoulder," Isaac called back. "I can still shoot with one hand."

The fight continued for the next half-hour. During that time, one of Ritter's men managed to catch the hay in the barn on fire. In only minutes, the structure was fully ablaze. Pa moved us boys to the back of the house.

"We're gettin' low on ammo, Pa," Isaac told him. "We've hit a few of them, but there're just too many."

Pa listened for a moment. The rifle fire from Ritter's men didn't seem any less than when the fight started.

"All right, boys. We gotta let 'em have the house. Are the horses back in the trees?"

"Yes, Daddy." I stepped up to him. "But do we have to let 'em win?"

"Sometimes, it's better to withdraw and fight again. That's what we're gonna do. Now, go to the horses."

"What about you?" I tried, but failed, to keep the fear out of my voice.

"I'll be along. I'm gonna stay a few minutes while y'all get to the horses. Don't want those boys out there to know we're leavin'." He gave me a tiny shove. "Now, get goin'."

We all got to the horses. I helped Isaac climb into his saddle. Then Pa rushed up, holding his side. In the dark, we couldn't see the blood.

As soon as Pa was on his horse, we took off. Ritter's men were still shootin' at the house.

For the next ten minutes, we followed Pa through the trees and brush behind the house. The trail he rode trended uphill until we topped out on a ridge. Pa stopped us for a breather.

"They're comin'," he said after watchin' our back trail for a few minutes.

We set off again. In a few more minutes, we emerged from the trees onto a long, flat prairie. We took off across it at a gallop.

About halfway across, I glanced back and saw riders burst from the trees behind us. "Pa!" I yelled. When he looked back, I pointed at the riders.

Another glance showed me they were shootin'. Even I knew they were too far off.

We ran the horses for an hour as fast as they could run. Before long, they began showing signs of givin' out.

*****

That brought me back to the rocks and trees where we hid now. Wiping sweat from my forehead, I looked back out over the small open meadow in front of the rocks. Nobody comin' yet.

Five minutes later, Isaac called out, "Here they come!"

"Make sure of your shots, boys. We're low on bullets." Pa stared out over the rocks, his face creased by pain and worry.

The riders came on, not knowin' we were in the rocks. Pa waited until they were within fifty yards of us before takin' the first shot.

We emptied four saddles in that first volley of firin'. The other riders pulled back out of good range.

"Anybody hit?" Pa called out.

"I think we're all in one piece," Isaac replied.

"They'll try sneakin' up on us now," Moses said. "Try to get in range and pick us off."

Pa nodded. "I think you're right. Keep a sharp watch. If you see one of 'em and can get a good shot, take it. These boys ain't playin'. Well, neither are we."

He went back in the trees then and called me to him. "Mac, help me look at these holes those boys put in me."

We took off his shirt. When the tails we pushed in pulled out of the holes in his side, the bleedin' started again.

"Pa, you're bleedin' too much." I swiped at the blood with his shirt.

He sat down and leaned back against a tree. The way he looked scared me. "Go look in my saddlebags and bring one of those clean shirts. I'm gonna rest here for a minute."

That scared me even more. Pa never rested in the middle of the day, no matter how tired he was. I got the shirt and returned.

As I came up close, I stopped. With his eyes closed like they were, he looked like he was dead. Then his eyes opened.

"Mac, I'm gonna ask you to do a real hard thing." Pa looked at me real hard. "I want you to get on your horse and ride out of here the back way."

"No, Pa! I ain't gonna leave you!"

"You got to, son. We ain't gonna leave here. You can get away and live."

"Pa..."

"No, boy. You got to do it. Do it for your ma. Ride to Mexico to her family. Ride down this canyon, take the trail to the right. It'll take you to a good road that goes right to your ma's family ranch." He took a deep breath. "Do it for me, son."

With tears slicking my cheeks, I nodded. On my horse at the end of the canyon, I heard the shots start up again.

The End

Made in the USA
San Bernardino, CA
23 December 2018